SAD SONG OF THE WHALE

Anthony Masters

Before them lay the vast body of a whale, looking jaundiced in the moonlight, its torn and bloodied lips still compressed in a curl of a grin. Its flesh had been slashed and taut wires had been hooked around the enormous swathes.

Tim is the newest member of Green Watch – an environmental pressure group founded by his uncle, Scb Howard, and his two kids, Brian and Flower. Together they battle to protect the natural world from ruthless exploitation – campaigning against the needless slaughter of innocent creatures and the thoughtless pollution of the environment. No animal is too small for Green Watch to care about and no place too remote for them to get too. Needless to say, they manage to ruffle quite a few feathers along the way . . .

Also in the Green Watch series:

Battle For The Badgers by Anthony Masters

SAD SONG OF THE WHALE

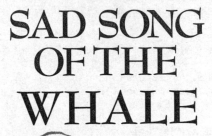

Book Two in the Green Watch series

Debbie

by
Anthony Masters
Illustrated by Pauline Hazelwood

Hippo Books
Scholastic Publications Limited
London

Scholastic Publications Ltd.,
10 Earlham Street, London WC2H 9RX, UK

Scholastic Inc.,
730 Broadway, New York, NY 10003, USA

Scholastic Tab Publications Ltd.,
123 Newkirk Road, Richmond Hill,
Ontario L4C 3G5, Canada

Ashton Scholastic Pty Ltd.,
P O Box 579, Gosford, New South Wales,
Australia

Ashton Scholastic Ltd.,
165 Marua Road, Panmure, Auckland 6,
New Zealand

First published in the UK by Scholastic Publications Ltd., 1990

Copyright © Anthony Masters, 1990
Illustration copyright © Pauline Hazelwood, 1990

ISBN 0 590 76348 2

Typeset by AKM Associates (UK) Ltd, Southall, London
Printed by Cox and Wyman Ltd., Reading, Berks

Chapter One

"It's a humpback," yelled Seb.

"Where?" Tim stared out at the monstrous grey expanse of the South Atlantic. "I can't see anything."

"*There*," said Flower firmly. "Use your eyes."

Then he saw it – huge, magnificent, sleekly gliding through the waves, curiously part of the ocean, mysteriously adapting itself to the water's flow.

"Blimey," said Tim. "It's vast."

Brian put his binoculars down on the *Sea Serpent*'s bridge table. The old motor torpedo boat lurched and wallowed in the trough of the waves, so that they lost sight of the whale for frustrating seconds while icy spray flung itself at the thickened glass, making visibility even more difficult.

Despite the elements the whale scudded along,

1

almost sinuous in the watery folds. Then it was gone – out of sight but not out of mind. Tim shivered. He had been feeling cold and despondent and bone-weary in the shaking old ship, but now life had a purpose. Again. He had seen the creature they had come to save.

Later, in the poky saloon that smelt of diesel oil and grease and yesterday's stew, Seb told him more. Tim felt ignorant, conscious of the fact that Flower and Brian must know so much more than he did. After all, they had been out here before. They had seen the whales.

"Where did they come from?" he asked Seb. "I mean, in the beginning."

They were sipping the skipper's strong tea with condensed milk. It had taken some getting used to, but now it was oddly comforting.

"Well, they're mammals. At some point, thousands – millions – of years before the dawn of man, they went into the sea. Just walked into the water." Seb grinned. "Don't ask me how or why, I just don't know."

"Ancient mysteries," said Flower.

"Dawn of time." Brian yawned.

"Don't spoil it," snapped Tim. He knew the founder members of Green Watch well enough now to criticize them – except Seb, of course. He was still slightly in awe of Flower and Brian's unpredictable father.

"You should hear their music, though," Seb continued.

"That's the great bit," said Brian. His eyes lit up and he exchanged a look with his father that was one of pure elation. Tim suddenly felt left out until a hand gently squeezed his shoulder. It was Flower.

"Don't worry," she said. "You'll hear it. Look forward to hearing it. It's magic."

"It's got a sort of ethereal quality," Seb went on. "Even when you hear it through an iron hull."

"It's magic."

Tim looked up at her wonderingly. He had never known her in a mood like this. Usually she was practical, fiercely independent. But now he could see that she had a kind of yearning inside her.

Seb muttered, "Listen to this," and began quoting from *Whale Nation* by Heathcote Williams.

"Great stuff, isn't it? And he's right. It sounds just like that. Even with an iron hull."

"What's this? You calling my ship names?"

Liam Miles was not exactly how Tim had imagined an ex-whaling skipper. He was a short, stocky man, clean shaven, and looked rather like a bank clerk, or the stereotype of a bank clerk. He was very neat, very precise in his speech and movements, and he kept the old motor torpedo boat in sparkling condition, which was pretty amazing considering that, in addition to Green Watch, he had only two crew members: Scotty, a tall silent man who spoke, illogically, with an Irish accent, and Harold, who also stood in as the ship's cook and was as talkative as Scotty was taciturn. It was rumoured that Harold, built like a tank, had a violent temper but

Tim, fortunately, had not seen it. Yet.

"No," said Seb, "I'm simply reminding everybody they can hear the whales singing here."

"Yes," said Liam, the look in his eyes softening. "You certainly can."

All that Tim knew about Liam Miles was that he used to be a whaling skipper and that he was now a conservationist, battling to save the creatures he had previously hunted. His opponents were an international fishing group with a small factory ship. Legally they were no longer allowed to hunt the whales so many miles offshore, but they continually flouted the law and no one seemed to be interested in enforcing it. At the moment Green Watch were monitoring the situation.

"Tim –"

"Eh?"

"He's drifted off," said Brian. "Hypnotized by whale magic. Gone into a whale trance."

Tim threw an apple at him but Brian first ducked and then leapt and caught it.

That's the trouble with Brian, thought Tim: he looks a right little bookworm but in fact he's good at everything. It isn't fair.

"I think we have trouble," said Liam suddenly.

"What trouble?" asked Seb quickly. The atmosphere instantly changed and a little pulse beat in Seb's temple.

"A catcher – at least I think it is. We're picking her up on the radar and she seems to be closing in." He paused and then spoke with more than his usual

4

precision. "It'll take a while before she overtakes us, but we're not likely to outrun her."

After a lunch of rather heavy bean stew, Tim went to lie down on the bunk in his tiny, narrow cabin. They had been at sea for about thirty-six hours now and he was proud that he hadn't felt sick at all, despite the pitching and swaying of the ancient *Sea Serpent*. But he was prouder still that Seb had included him in the expedition, that he had phoned his mother and actually persuaded her to let him come. He would never forget the conversation he had had with her just after the call. She had come up to his bedroom, looking thoroughly bemused.

"I mean," she had said, "he wants you to go. All the way out there."

"Who wants me to go?"

"That no good brother of your dad's. That man who got you into all that trouble with those badgers and that man Mr Andrews and that awful Mr Johnson.* The time you almost got shot. Remember?" She paused triumphantly, waiting for him to deny it all.

"That's a bit of an exagger–"

"And now he wants you to go. All the way out there."

"You mean Seb phoned, and wants me to – to go *where*, Mum?" Tim was in an agony of delighted suspense. It was months since he had seen his

---

* *Battle for the Badgers*. Book One in the Green Watch series.

extraordinary cousins and shared with them the equally extraordinary adventure that had made him a member of Green Watch. And now – what was she trying to say?

"He wants you to go to the Falklands, Tim. I've never heard such a cheek."

"It *is* the Easter holidays, Mum. And only the beginning."

"And how long's he going to keep you out there? That's what I want to know."

"What does he want me to do?"

"Go to the Falklands. I said –"

Tim suppressed a wave of irritation. Why couldn't she ever get to the point? Since his dad had been in prison, his mother seemed to have got worse. She'd had a breakdown, which wasn't really surprising, but now she rambled all the time and couldn't make any decisions at all. "What does he want me to *do*?"

"Protect some whales."

"Wow!"

"I wasn't having you out there. Mixed up with whales now – after all that trouble with the badgers and the engines. I mean, what does he expect?" Then her voice faltered. "Trouble is, he talked me into it."

"Mum. That's fantastic."

"It's awful. I don't know what got into me."

Tim threw his arms around her. "I love you, Mum."

"You want to get away from me, you mean."

"What did he say? When am I going? How shall I get there? What about –"

6

His mother held up her hands in a long-suffering gesture, but suddenly she was smiling. "I must admit – despite everything – I felt proud of you, Tim."

"Why?"

"It was what he said. That you'd been a brave boy and they needed you. Needed you because you were a member of Green Watch."

Tim felt as if his heart was going to burst with pride. Wouldn't he always look back and see these moments as the happiest of his life?

"Of course I shouldn't let you go. But after what those newspapers said last time. About how well Green Watch had –"

"Mum?"

"Yes, love?"

"Can I really go? I mean if you're going to be lonely –"

"It's not that." She swallowed. "It's the danger."

"If you're going to worry I *won't* go," said Tim uneasily.

"No. It does so much for your dad. I *want* you to go."

"Does it really?"

"You know it does. He's proud of you. You can see it in his face. It's giving your dad something to live for, knowing you're in this Green Watch thing. He talks to the other prisoners about it – and he grows bigger, Tim. And stronger. In his heart. Do you know what I mean?"

Tim nodded. "So I'm going?"

"If you want. Seb's going to come and pick you up the day after tomorrow."

"Blimey."

"Well, he always moves fast. He's coming with Brian and Flower, those two smarty-pants kids of his. They're going to fly from Brize Norton on an RAF plane and end up in Port Stanley. It's an awfully long flight."

"I don't mind."

"He'll tell you the rest. He's going to phone again tonight. I've got to get you kitted out and we'll have to . . ."

The conversation filtered back in every detail as Tim dozed. The flight, Port Stanley and the *Sea Serpent*, however, seemed to merge together in one frantic wilderness that was so beautiful it took his breath away – and was sometimes so frightening that he had desperately wanted to be back in the safety of his own home. But at least he hadn't been sick.

"Tim –"

"Mm?"

"Tim."

It was Flower, leaning over him, smelling of salt and wind. "It's time to get up."

Tim yawned and stretched. Although she was his own age, Flower always seemed to be older, much older than him. It wasn't that they weren't good friends – and they had been through so much together – but she always seemed so very much in charge.

"What's happening?"

"It's a bit dodgy. That boat's closing in."

"The whaler?"

"Yes." For the first time since he had met her Tim saw real fear in her eyes. It gave him a shock to realize that she could feel vulnerable too. "Dad says we're not to try to outrun her. And Liam agrees."

It struck Tim that the roles seemed to have been reversed. Shouldn't Liam be giving the orders? Not agreeing with Seb? But he knew all too well the steely authority that Seb could muster on occasion. After all, he had experienced it himself. But why was Flower so afraid?

"What can they do, anyway?" he asked.

"I don't know. But they've attacked people before."

"Flower –"

"Yes?"

"I've never seen you scared."

"Thanks, that helps a lot."

"Seriously."

She looked away from him. "It's just all this." She stared out of the porthole at the grey expanse that lay beyond. "It's such a wilderness."

"I thought you'd been out here before."

"We have. But we weren't out at sea like this. Not for such a long time."

"Who's in charge? Liam or Seb?" asked Tim suddenly.

"Liam's the skipper. But Dad's financing him to watch where the whalers are and radio up the fishery protection people."

"Shouldn't they be looking anyway? Not us."

"They don't bother to enforce the law. You know all this. Seb told you." She looked at him impatiently.

Tim nodded. "Yes, I know."

"Then why are you getting me to repeat it all?"

Tim hesitated. "I thought, if I kept you talking, you might not be so scared," he said at last.

She looked at him and Tim could see there was a sudden, immense gratitude in her eyes.

"Tim." She took his hand.

"Yes?" he asked, almost fearfully.

"Thanks. I'm being a fool. Brian wouldn't understand."

"Of course he would," said Tim loyally.

"No, he's too like Dad."

"What's that meant to mean?"

"It means he's too single-minded. They both just think about the job in hand – not the consequences."

"And Liam?"

"He's afraid too. I can feel it. I don't know about Scotty and Harold."

"So what are you afraid of?" asked Tim, almost belligerently.

Again she looked out of the porthole at the heaving grey sea. "All that. The thought of being in it – of being sucked down. It would be so cold."

"You're telling me!"

"Don't laugh."

"I'm not."

She got up and Tim tumbled out of his bunk behind her. "I'm sorry. Don't go."

"I feel a fool."

"No. It's me who's a fool. Honest. I just haven't got any imagination."

Flower laughed sharply. It was a harsh barking sound. "What do you mean?"

"Ever since I got here, it's been like magic. And everything's happened so fast, I haven't caught up with it." He paused and she began edging away from him. "Wait! Wait a minute!" Tim was desperate not to let her go. Somehow he knew that if he could reach Flower now it would establish a new stage in their friendship. A good stage, one he wanted.

"Well?"

"Is it the sea?"

"I told you it was, you idiot."

"Or is it Seb, and Brian?"

"What do you mean? They're not afraid."

"But that's what I mean. You're alone."

"Rubbish."

"It's true." Tim was almost triumphant. "It's like me, when I first met you all and we were climbing. Do you remember? I got stuck because I was so scared and clung to that cliff like a limpet. I've never felt so alone."

"We probably didn't help you much."

"You did. Afterwards."

"Dad's always taught us to face up to things. But I can't this time. It's too awful. It's as if the sea's a pit – a sort of sucking pit."

"Can't you talk to him about it?"

"No."

"Why not?"

"Because I'd feel weak. It would *weaken* me to talk to him about it."

"Seb wouldn't want you to feel like that. Surely?"

"No."

"Then why –?"

"Because I'd feel *weak*," she said again. "Don't you see?" She was quite angry now. For the life of him Tim couldn't really understand. Why couldn't she talk to her father?

"Talk to me," he said then. There was a pause. "Talk to *me*," he repeated urgently. "Don't you want to?"

After a moment Flower nodded. "I'd like to try," she said softly. "It's just that – I've always been afraid of water. Always."

"Like I've been afraid of heights?"

"Yes. I can – I can feel that boat coming towards me. And then something will happen and we'll all spill into the sea." Her voice ended on a hard, dry sob.

"They wouldn't ram us," said Tim. "I mean, what can they do to us? Nothing." He sounded very sure but deep inside he wasn't.

"They could say it was an accident." Flower shivered. "Don't you realize, if we really make trouble for them – if we can really get the law enforced against them – they're going to lose thousands of pounds, maybe their livelihood. So if they can get rid of us –"

"What do you mean, get rid of us?"

12

"If we were all drowned," her voice rose shakily, "there'd be no one to make trouble for them. Would there?"

"It won't come to that," Tim protested feebly.

"Won't it?" She stared at him defiantly.

"Talk it over with Seb," Tim pressed her.

"I've already told you," she replied flatly. "He wouldn't understand."

But Tim thought he would.

Chapter Two

The *Sea Serpent* did not live up to her name. She was small, stubby, squat and oily. Her decks were short and she had a bulbous superstructure that made her look top-heavy. Tim wondered if Liam Miles was fond of her – or just regarded the *Sea Serpent* as part of his equipment.

It was cold on deck and the sea was a heaving grey-green mass. Its very immensity had originally frightened him as much as it did Flower, but today, with *Sea Serpent* wallowing so heavily in the troughs, its danger had seemed more remote. In fact he had begun to enjoy being bumped about on its monstrous surface, and the first sight of the whale had been incredible. They were primeval beings all right, with nothing fish-like about them at all. He could imagine them as vast limbed creatures roaming the earth. They were beasts of the early ages, the real owners of the earth, now refugees at sea. Leaning on the rail, Tim stared at the horizon, hoping for another sighting of the dancing, gliding whale that was now as much a part of the sea as it had originally been of the land.

Then he saw a smudge. It wasn't a whale, couldn't be, for it was quite the wrong shape. Jagged, indistinct, it was definitely a ship. Suddenly he felt a surge of excitement followed by a tingling kind of dread. Was this the catcher?

"OK, we have her."

"Is it the catcher?" Tim was breathless as he arrived on the bridge.

Seb and Liam were staring out over the ship's port side while Scotty was at the helm. Brian was sitting at the chart table reading a book and looking, as usual, totally unconcerned, while Flower held on to the back of the captain's chair, her knuckles showing white. But when Seb turned round she released the chair, looking her old relaxed self. Tim felt a stab of pain. Why couldn't Seb understand how afraid she was? Beneath all his steely armour he was an emotional man. Tim had even seen him cry.

"It's called the *Fortune of War*," said Liam, "and heading straight for us." He picked up the intercom. "Harold, I want you up here. No, I don't care what you're making in the galley. I want you up here now." He grinned at Tim. "That man would insist on going down with his ship if he was in the middle of making a suet pudding."

"Are we making contact with her?" asked Seb.

"Let's see what she does. I'm going to alter course."

But after a while it became ominously clear that the *Fortune of War* had altered course too, and was steering straight for their bows.

"Will she ram us?" asked Brian, looking up from his book. He isn't that cool, thought Tim, but he's a surprising person. He rarely shows his emotions but when it comes to action he's as quick and decisive as his father and sister.

Tim often wondered what damage had been done when Mrs Howard walked out just as Seb was getting Green Watch off the ground. Obviously she hadn't been able to take it; maybe she had even felt excluded. Once Flower had told him that her mother had been a better climber than her father, and that Seb hadn't wanted to compete with her and had shut her out of Green Watch. It was the only time she had mentioned her mother. She had suddenly seemed to want to confide in him, immediately after their first adventure, just before Tim had left to go back to London. But now, of course, she was confiding in him in a very different way.

No one answered immediately. Then Liam said, "Of course she won't but she may try to communicate."

Sure enough, the radio crackled into life a few minutes later. "This is *Fortune of War* calling *Sea*

16

Serpent. Fortune of War calling *Sea Serpent*. Are you receiving us? Over."

"This is *Sea Serpent*," replied Seb into the mike. "We're receiving you. Over."

"This is *Fortune of War*. You are interrupting our operations. Your vessel is too close. Over."

"You shouldn't be whaling here in the first place," cut in Liam. "You're not allowed in these waters. Over."

"Are you a conservation group?" The voice was educated, slightly foreign, but the speaker's English was excellent.

"Yes. We are called Green Watch. Over."

"I don't think I've heard of you. Over." The tone was patient and courteous but there was a slightly mocking edge to it.

"We're small," said Liam. "But committed."

"My name is Captain Stanton. I'm in charge of this operation, and of the factory ship *Maid of the Sea*, and we have some weeks to go. We don't want trouble. Over."

"Then stop."

"Very impractical, Captain –?"

"Captain Miles. I have observers on board. I would like to point out that you are in contravention of the 1982 Whaling Act. I shall be reporting you to the Commission. And we shall continue to observe. Over."

"You are welcome to observe. But if you come any closer your ship will hamper our operations."

"That, of course, would be most unfortunate," said Liam smoothly.

"If you continue to do this, you are running the risk of an accident."

"Are you threatening me, Captain? Over."

"I am simply pointing out that you are in contravention yourselves – of the most elementary safety rules at sea, and risk collision. Over."

"We are observing only. Over."

There was a long pause while the *Fortune of War* continued to head towards them. She seemed to be very close now. Liam and Seb looked grimly ahead at the encroaching whaler while Tim again saw Flower clutch the chair.

"Are they going to veer off?"

No one answered Brian's calm question and he sighed and went back to his book. Was this Stanton man bluffing, Tim wondered. Or was he really on course for the *Sea Serpent*?

"Talking of safety," said Liam into the radio. "Aren't you getting a little close? Over."

"Captain Miles, this is my last word. Keep your conscience and your ship out of our way. Over and out."

Still the *Fortune of War* came on. Suddenly Flower let out a little whimper which she tried unsuccessfully to turn into a cough. Brian gave her a curious look but Seb had eyes only for the *Fortune of War*. At the last moment she changed course and Tim let out a sigh of relief.

"You didn't think she was going to hit us, did you?" asked Brian.

"Oh no," replied Tim with an effort. "Of course not." Out of the corner of his eye he saw Flower crumple into a chair.

"So what's the plan of campaign?" asked Liam.

Green Watch were sitting over a lunch of rather overdone baked beans and spam fritters. The sea was running calm now and a cold orange sun rode high in the pale sky.

"I think we should carry on as before: photograph them off limits, follow them down to South Georgia and then head back with the evidence. We haven't managed to photograph a kill yet, but if we can hang on for another couple of days we're bound to. The factory ship's somewhere off South Georgia now."

"I'm risking the ship," said Liam.

"That's why you bought her," Seb reminded him firmly.

Scotty looked up from his beans. "Worth the risk, I reckon," he said briefly. "Whaling sickens you in the end. We all know that."

"Were you all whalers?" asked Tim.

"Sure." Harold leant back, looking at him quizzically. "We all were once. But then something happened." He paused. "You won't believe us."

"Let me tell the story," said Liam. "Then maybe he will. Scotty and Harold and I were on a catcher boat, like the *Fortune of War*. As soon as the factory ship detected the shape of a whale on underwater radar we got sent out. You probably noticed the harpoon on the raised foredeck of the *Fortune of War*.

Well, you swivel that in the direction of the whale, wait till it comes within range, switch off the engines and wait some more. When the whale surfaces you fire, trying to get an accurate shot between its shoulder blades with the harpoon gun. But if you miss, you fire again, and again. Anyway, it was a routine. It was good money and none of us had any roots back on shore." He paused. "There was a lot of fog and ice about one morning but we still took the catcher out because a whale had been detected. In the lousy conditions we hit a berg – a small one, but enough to damage us badly. The radio packed up and the fog and ice closed in. We thought we'd had it. Then we heard something; whether it was bouncing off our hull or the berg, I don't know. Of course I'd heard it before, but it was so near this time. It sounded something like you imagine a siren's song – you know, the music that was supposed to lead sailors on to the rocks. But this sounded reassuring some-how. We were leaking like a sieve and the pumps were useless. If we could only get to one of the islands – even South Georgia – I knew we'd stand a chance. But I hadn't the faintest idea how to get through the ice without another collision." He paused again and Tim could see that everyone was riveted. "The whale surfaced about fifty yards away and then slowly swam ahead of us. We followed, still leaking like a sieve. We seemed to follow him for an eternity, through the ice flews and the fog. But we never lost him. And he never lost us. The pumps began holding their own and we landed on South Georgia. I remember the whale left us just as we sighted land." Liam looked round the table doubtfully. "It was all just one big coincidence, wasn't it? No more, no less."

Tim didn't know what to think and, glancing at the others, he sensed that Seb and Flower and Brian were as sceptical as he was. It was one of those stories . . .

Then Harold said quietly, "I know what you're thinking. Maybe we feel the same. But I'll tell you this: once I got back on the factory ship and saw the minced whale flesh being shoved into the digestion tanks to be boiled down I felt like throwing up. And the money didn't matter any more. We all seemed to have come to the same decision."

Scotty nodded. "You bet we did. It just hit us: what the hell were we doing this lousy job for?"

Then Liam took up the story again. "We split up and went back to land. I got a job as an electrician, Harold as a cook in a greasy spoon restaurant –"

"It was a fish bar," protested Harold.

"And Scotty as a garage mechanic. But none of us could get that whale out of our minds. I mean we used to meet. Have reunions. Get drunk. And talk about whales – as if they were some kind of magical talisman. Then we met Seb in the Falklands. Trying to do what you're all doing now, but without a boat."

"Yes," said Seb, "it was a little frustrating. All I did was to hitch rides and sound off."

"Anyway, we'd come to the Falklands – all three of us – to get away from the boring jobs we'd got. Thought we'd try a little sheep farming. It'd been all right, quite a bit of fun, in fact. But when Seb managed to lease the *Sea Serpent* and told me what he wanted us to do, all the magic came back. We owed the whales one, we reckoned. And we still do."

"So we're going to hang around, are we, Dad?" asked Brian. There was a rare note of excitement in his voice. "Hang around and take some more photographs. I can use my new camera."

"The computer one?" There was relief in Flower's voice. The immediate danger was over.

All the next day the *Sea Serpent* continued on its course towards the factory ship. When they finally spotted her in a haze of afternoon sunset, she looked as big as an aircraft carrier. Tim was overwhelmed.

"A floating slaughterhouse," said Seb. His eyes were pinned intently on her and there was a look of fierce anger on his face. "If only I could blow her out of the sea instead of taking damn photographs."

Liam grinned. "We think you'll be more useful outside jail."

"They're off limits," growled Seb. "Miles off limits. There won't be a whale left in the ocean after they've finished."

That night they played cards, tossed around on a rolling sea in their warm and cosily lit little cabin. But later Tim was quite unable to sleep. He was used to the motion now, but he couldn't stop worrying about Flower. Superficially she was her old self, laughing and joking with everyone. But he could still detect the despair inside her.

22

At six, still unable to do more than doze, he got up and went up to the bridge where Liam was on watch.

"Can't sleep?"

"No."

"Cocoa?"

"Great." He clasped the warm cup that Liam handed him and sipped at its sweet, dark contents.

"Good time, dawn," said Liam. "Makes you feel you can cope with things."

"I haven't seen many of them," admitted Tim.

Liam laughed. "I don't s'pose you have." He stared ahead. "There's ice up there. Floating pack ice and the bigger stuff."

"Bergs?"

"Yes, and mighty big ones."

"And they'll send off the catcher boats through that?"

"No, they'll keep clear. But those big bergs might be useful if we have to run for cover."

"So you think they'll damage us?"

"If we stopped shouting, life would be much easier for them."

"Don't other conservation groups do anything?"

"Oh yes. Look at all those Greenpeace leaflets. And they're out there contesting them too. We're not alone. They daren't touch Greenpeace, though. They're too big. But if we had an accident, it might serve as a warning."

"So –"

"We have to keep our wits about us, Tim. And by the way, Flower's up too."

"Flower?"

"Couldn't sleep, like you. Not for most of the night."

"Where is she?"

"Prowling about on deck."

Tim hurried down the companionway ladder to find Flower in an anorak, shivering and gazing out over the sea.

"What are you doing?" he asked.

"Having a look."

"What at?"

"The sea, you prat."

"Why? I thought you were –"

"Scared? I am. But I figured if I kept on looking at it, I might get less scared."

Tim laughed with delight and affection.

"You're laughing at me now," she said indignantly.

"I'm not laughing. I really admire you. You've got guts. Loads of guts."

"Not out here, I haven't. I've done so many things. Never worried. Never gave them a second thought. But this –"

"I know how hard you're trying, Flower. *And* how some things seem quite impossible."

She turned away from him. "You have to keep trying. That's what Dad taught me."

Tim felt a sudden, sharp pang. His dad wouldn't be out of prison for another two years yet. And there was nothing he could teach him.

At breakfast, the sea was the calmest they had seen it

yet. Seb seemed tired, almost jaundiced by the expedition, but Brian could obviously detect a light of battle glimmering in his father's eye.

"What are you up to, Dad?"

"What do you mean, Brian?" He looked all innocence, but Liam also seemed aware of an under-current. "Come on, Seb. You've got that shifty look. What do you want to do?"

"Well, we've photographed from a distance and there's no doubt that we can prove they're off limits, though what good that will do I don't know. But if we manage to take some close-ups of the harpooning – and we could get them on board the factory ship – then we'd have some pretty remarkable press pictures."

Scotty laughed. "You mean –"

"I mean we'd stand a damn sight better chance if we woke up Joe Public."

"How would we get on the factory ship, Dad?" asked Brian.

"Well, it's risky. Getting close. They'd have every excuse to run us down. But if I took the life raft at night and ran up a line to the deck, we could be in business."

"Boarding her?" asked Tim incredulously. "That's a bit of a risk, isn't it?"

But Flower was grinning. "Who's going with you, Dad? I mean, you'll need some help, won't you?"

"Yes. I'll take Liam."

"That's great, isn't it?" snapped Brian. "Why bother to bring us if you don't trust us? We're just kids, aren't we? Not really part of Green Watch at all."

Seb stared at him, knowing that they had reached the impasse he had been dreading for so long. Just how far could he really involve them? That's what they were all wondering right now.

"All right." Seb was almost whispering. "I'll take one of you, and we'll do it by choosing straws. OK?"

"OK," said Flower, and Brian instantly looked more cheerful. But Tim was afraid. Was Seb really proposing to mix them up in such a dangerous episode? What would his parents think? Tim could imagine his mum raving and storming about "that man". But his dad was an unknown quantity. Maybe he would approve.

Seb went to fetch some matches. He broke one of them in two and then placed them between his fingers.

"Choose," he said quietly.

A thrill of fear mixed with anticipation ran through Tim's veins.

Flower chose first. She took the match firmly, without hesitation. It was unbroken and she gave her father a look of angry disappointment. Then Tim chose, and when he pulled the match out of Seb's fingers it was broken.

"Blimey," he gulped, turning to Brian, who said calmly.

"You can swop if you don't fancy –"

"No, he can't," rapped Seb fiercely.

"No, I won't," said Tim unhappily.

Seb went to his camera case and pulled out what looked like a wristwatch. He gave it to Tim. "Strap it on. Whenever you stretch out or hold up your hand it'll take a photograph."

"So I go round stretching out and holding up my hand?" Tim was horrified. "Won't that look suspicious?"

Seb laughed. "Hopefully we won't be seen. OK, there'll be security men around, but we'll just have to avoid them."

"You're taking one hell of a risk," said Brian. "What happens if you get caught?"

"The worst that can happen is they ask us to leave." Seb sounded confident. "After all, we're only protesters."

Brian didn't seem so sure and Flower said, "Dad –"

"Well?"

"Aren't you pushing this one a bit too hard?"

"Maybe," he replied slowly. "We'll just have to play it by ear." It was not a remark that comforted Tim.

"Something else," said Seb.

"For me to do?" stuttered Tim in alarm.

"No, this one's for me. While we're on board I intend to make a gesture which you'll photograph, Tim. There's a built-in flash on that camera."

"A V sign?" asked Brian mildly.

"No," replied Seb, "something a bit more positive. I've been wanting to use this for a long time." He went to a locker and got out a banner. "Providing I can get to a strategic point on the *Maid of the Sea*, I intend to unfurl it, have Tim photograph it and then mail the picture back to the British press. It should get us a good headline – something like GREEN WATCH INVADE FACTORY SHIP."

Tim felt a stab of rising panic. Seb wasn't grinning now; he was shaking with a fury that Tim had never seen him display before, a kind of deep-down anger that was really frightening to see. Had he been as committed as this with the badgers? With Mr Andrews? Surely not. Or was he just worn out? Ill even? Tim took another look at Seb's face. There was something about his expression that nearly froze him to the spot. He glanced at Brian and Flower, but they didn't seem to have noticed anything unusual at all.

Then Liam came in and Seb began eagerly explaining to him what he intended to do. As he spoke, he unfurled the huge green banner, laying it out with some difficulty on the floor.

"Seb." Liam's voice was hard and unyielding.

"Mmm."

The banner now lay, fully open, across the floor. Its wording read: STOP WHALE SLAUGHTER NOW. YOU ARE FISHING ILLEGALLY.

"Seb."

"What is it, Liam?"

"Don't you think you're rushing into all this?"

"Rushing?" He looked up incredulously. "I'm seizing an opportunity."

"You don't think you're stretching an opportunity too far?"

"No."

"Taking young Tim into danger?"

"This is a demonstration, not a battle."

"I gather you had some rough stuff last time."

"That was last time," said Seb dismissively.

"We didn't mind," Tim put in, trying to be helpful, but Liam was frowning now and he could feel the tension between the two men mounting.

"So you propose to board that factory ship with your nephew and run both of you into danger? What do you suppose his parents would think? And what does Tim really feel?"

"I want to go," said Tim doggedly.

Liam continued relentlessly, "I think you're completely irresponsible."

"We're in the risk business."

"You have three kids."

"*They're* in the risk business."

"Rubbish."

"I think you're wrong, Seb." Liam's voice was bitter.

"I'll be the judge of that."

"Not while I'm the captain of this ship."

"*What?*"

"While I'm captain of the *Sea Serpent* I forbid you to put any of these children's lives at risk."

"I'm expedition leader," began Seb.

They were being damn childish, thought Tim, both of them. But neither Seb nor Liam were going to back off, he could see that.

"Seb –" Liam tried to sound more placating.

"We're going ahead," replied Seb quietly.

"No, you're not," snapped Liam.

There was a short silence but to Tim it seemed to go on for ever. Again he glanced at Brian and Flower. They were looking curious rather than strained; maybe they had never seen a confrontation between Seb and Liam before.

"Look –" Seb's voice was almost pleading. "We have to do *something*."

"We're doing enough."

"Ineffectively."

"It's *enough*. If you will involve your kids in Green Watch you can't carry on as if they were adults."

"Why not?" Seb stared at him in genuine bewilderment, as if the thought had never occurred to him before.

"They're kids. You're responsible for them."

Seb moved towards the door of the wheelhouse. "I'm sorry, Liam. We'll talk about this another time."

For a moment Tim thought that Liam was going to bar the door. Then he stepped back. "On your head be it."

"It always is." He turned to Tim. "We'll get some sleep, and then I'll wake you about two am."

Tim nodded, feeling very nervous now. He glanced across at Flower, but she looked away, and he wondered what she was thinking.

Seb had the banner tucked into his shirt, and although it made him slightly bulky, Tim didn't think he looked suspicious. He was more worried about the watch. He knew that it would function if he raised his right hand, but he wasn't sure exactly how far, and he was wondering if he had already taken a photograph of the bottom of the dinghy as he had reached out for a handhold. It was lurching to and fro at the bottom of the ladder and there was a heavy swell that made Tim very uneasy.

Seb started the outboard and they began to bounce.

The noise of the engine sounded horribly loud and the sea looked immense. The factory ship was a dark shape looming in front of them, its bulky superstructure barely lit by a pale moon. It was enormous and the pallid light made it look like a dark city, full of grim, sightless buildings.

Gradually they drew into her shadow. *Maid of the Sea* was painted in large letters along her bow and great gouts of rust, like some terrible plague, were spread unevenly up her side. Barnacles and weeds festooned her waterline, while higher up her paint was peeling, cracking like boils and lacerations on her bow.

The dinghy wallowed in the trough of a wave off her stern and Tim took a photograph. Then he saw a dark hole yawning in front of them, and the dinghy nudged its way through to an enormous hatch with a jetty inside.

"Where are we going?" asked Tim.

"I've got a line which I'm going to attach to that crane head. It's got knots in it. Reckon you can make it?"

Heights were not Tim's strong point but he nodded dumbly. Somehow he would have to do it. Without further enquiry, Seb threw up the line, which had a metal hook at the end of it. There was an awful click as the hook fastened itself on to the lower part of the crane. It looked a snug fit, but it also looked a long way up. Tim shuddered and he felt the sweat breaking out all over his body.

"Want to go first?" asked Seb.

Tim nodded and began the climb, determined not to look down. He felt a terrible lurch in his stomach as the space around him seemed to grasp at him, willing him to part company with the rope and to plunge into the chilling void. As he climbed Tim was also aware of an indefinable smell that seemed to pervade the ship. It was rank and cloying. That, and his fear, made the ascent a total nightmare, but he was conscious of Seb steadily hauling himself up behind him. He couldn't let him down now, Tim thought – couldn't fall – and somehow he continued to climb until he reached the deck. He grabbed a handhold and with an incredible sense of relief pulled himself up the final foot.

Then, as if this were quite a casual conversation, as if they were back on board their own ship, as if neither time nor security guards mattered in the slightest, Seb began a whispered account of how the factory ship worked. Tim could only marvel at the coolness and nerve of his companion.

"They have the capacity to deal with one whale every thirty minutes. When the whale's harpooned they come alongside and bore a hole into the nearest end of the body. Then they attach a towline and the poor creature's hauled to the bottom of the ramp where they make it fast and then pull it up the rope to the flensing deck. Next comes the messy part. The flensing crew start slicing the whale up and the flesh goes through a manhole to be cut up further by a machine. The product of that goes into digestive tanks and is boiled down by superheated steam while the whale oil is pumped into a separate house, goes through various processes and is then hardened up into edible fats, graded, barrelled and stored."

"And what's left?" asked Tim quietly. "It all sounds revolting."

"Well, they still have the skull, jawbones, ribs, spine and pelvis on deck, and so they're cut up and ground down, cooked and turned into fertilizer and chicken feed. There are dozens of uses for the whale. I won't go into them all now."

Just as well, thought Tim, who was wondering what was going to happen when they were discovered – which they surely would be any moment now. Didn't Seb have any nerves at all in his greyhound of a body?

"OK." Seb got to his feet at last. "Let's go."

Tim followed, grateful to be moving. They walked on down the deck and Tim gasped in horror at the sight that confronted them there. He turned to look at Seb. His face was set, expressionless, but his eyes were blazing with anger.

Before them lay the vast body of a whale, looking

jaundiced in the moonlight, its torn and bloodied lips still compressed in a curl of a grin. Its flesh had been slashed and taut wires had been hooked around the enormous swathes. For a second Tim had to look away as a wave of nausea swept over him. It was nothing but a massacre, and in his mind's eye he saw men hacking at the creature, men covered in blood and gore. Then he began to take photographs.

Seb went over to the whale and draped the banner across it, while Tim took more photographs. He had forgotten his fear of discovery now, forgotten the hellish descent awaiting him. All he could think of was the slaughter of this defenceless creature.

"Photograph everything you can see. How many shots have you got left?" asked Seb with sudden urgency.

"About twelve."

"OK, photograph those barrels, then some of that equipment over there. God knows what it is."

Tim quickly began to photograph. Just as he was nearing the end of his film Seb grabbed at him. "Behind the barrels. Now!"

But it was too late. The man had been standing watching them for a moment before Seb spotted him. Now he let out a loud yell and came lunging at Seb. Seb sidestepped him deftly, then with a neat chop to the back of the man's neck, knocked him out cold.

Leaving the man lying where he was, beside the body of the whale, Seb and Tim sped back down the deck to the crane head. They had no time to speculate on whether the man's shout had alerted any of his companions; and Tim had no time to agonize over the descent to the dinghy. His heart thumping painfully in his chest, and his breath coming in noisy little gasps, he slithered down the rope behind Seb, scarcely aware of what he was doing.

Only when Seb had started the dinghy and they were well clear of the factory ship's side did Tim look back. The ship reared up, dark and silent, and there was no evidence that they were being pursued. By some miracle, they had escaped.

Chapter Three

After Seb and Tim's narrow escape – and the success of their mission – breakfast that morning was a celebratory affair. Seb had his precious evidence and, though Stanton would be well aware by now that they had boarded his ship – illegally – he would have no way of proving it. But last night's episode had only strengthened Liam's case against Seb and there was still a tension between the two men.

Seb tried to ease it. "Liam, I'm sorry about our clash."

"Mmm."

"But we *did* succeed. We got the photographs."

"Sure."

"Isn't that important?"

"I don't like the kids' being involved. It's not right."

"I can't argue any more about that . . . ." Seb's voice was patient.

"Can I say something?" Tim asked Liam.

He shrugged.

"I could have ducked out. But I didn't."

"And you're old enough to make a decision like that?" snapped Liam.

"Yes," said Tim slowly.

"Liam –" Seb was hesitant for thc first time.

"What?"

"Are you going to stay with us?"

"Only if no more incidents like that occur."

"All right."

Liam stood up. "I'll give you another day – but that's it."

"It's a bargain." replied Seb.

That night Tim slept deeply. The events of the previous night had completely worn him out. But the elation he had felt on the factory ship – the complicity with Seb and Seb's wonderful determination – gave a new fillip to his involvement with Green Watch. What had been slow progress in a stunning new world had suddenly become something much more positive. The image of the flensing deck still haunted him and the smell seemed to have got right inside his head. Yet Tim felt satisfied. Surely when the photographs were developed and they appeared in the newspapers, there would be a public outcry? Then a still, small voice in his head told him that maybe the general public had seen many such pictures. All these various thoughts had been revolving in his mind as he drifted off to sleep.

He woke abruptly and for a moment wondered where he was. Then to his amazement Tim saw the door of his cabin was slightly ajar, and was now closing slowly. He struggled up on one elbow. Was someone in the room? Couldn't he hear movement? Breathing? Suddenly a hand was clamped over his mouth.

"Keep still," a rough voice hissed. Tim struggled and the hand increased its pressure until he could hardly breathe.

"If you stop struggling, I'll ease off."

Tim went limp.

"OK, now lie still or I'll kill you."

Tim didn't move.

"I want the film."

He shook his head and the pressure increased again.

"The film."

Tim was terrified, sweating, trying to nod, trying – and failing – to think ahead.

"The film."

He made a grunting sound.

"OK." The hand was released from his mouth. "But if you yell out, I swear to God I'll have you."

It was so wonderful to be able to breathe normally again that for a moment Tim forgot his fear.

"The film," the man whispered.

"I don't know. What film?"

"I sussed it out. That was a wristwatch job, wasn't it?"

"What *are* you talking about?"

"A wristwatch job. Camera on the watch. You raised your hand, I saw you. Bloody obvious to anyone who's used one."

"I don't know what you mean."

"Yes, you do."

"We came aboard for a demonstration."

"You came aboard to photograph." He grabbed Tim's wrist. "You cry out and I'll break it." He began to twist.

"No."

"Tell me then."

"I didn't –"

"Tell me." The pain was unbearable.

"OK."

"OK what?"

"I'll tell you." Relief flooded through him once more as the man released his wrist.

"Make it quick."

"I took a film."

"Where is it?"

"Someone else has got it."

"Who?"

"Seb. He took it out."

"So where is it?"

"In his cabin."

"OK, we'll soon fix that. You come with me."

"No."

"I said, you come –" He was holding something that gleamed suddenly in the moonlight. It was a knife.

"Which is his cabin?"

"Up the top."

"Move." They were standing in the narrow companionway. "Move, and don't open your mouth again," he snarled. Tim could hardly make out the man's shape. He was short and dressed in a black sweater and jeans. Just as they had left the cabin, Tim had looked up and seen the Balaclava mask. It had been a horrible sight: as if the man were faceless. "When we get to the door, you knock and ask if you can go in. I'll follow."

"OK."

They crept up the passage.

"Now."

Tim knocked once, and then once more.

"Who's there?" It was Seb's voice.

"Tim."

"What do you want?"

"I *must* see you."

"OK, the door's not locked."

Tim put his hand on the knob and pulled, and the door swung open.

"Well, come on in then." Seb sounded testy. "Can't you sleep, or what?"

"No." Tim was as tense as the man flattened behind the door. He could feel the knife point in his back. Then he made up his mind. "Seb, watch out," he yelled as he flung himself on to the floor.

"OK!" The man was diving for Tim's collar. "If you don't –"

But his words were cut short as with split-second timing Seb leapt from the bed and hurled himself at the intruder's body. Tim rolled to one side as they thrashed on the floor, with Seb's hands grappling for the knife. He was just wresting it away when the other man got a knee under him and kicked out. For a moment Seb lost control and fell backwards. As he did so, the man rolled over and was on his feet, tearing up the companionway as the other doors opened and startled heads popped out. Seb was still stunned and the man had launched himself up the companion ladder and disappeared on deck before he had time to recover. As Seb thudded up the ladder in his turn, Tim heard the roaring of an outboard engine. They had lost him.

"It's getting heavy," said Liam despondently as all seven Green Watch members sat round the galley table. "Too heavy."

"He obviously came from the factory ship," said Flower.

"Yes." Seb was still panting. "Are you OK, Tim?"

"Fine." Tim proceeded to tell them everything that had happened between him and the intruder. When he had finished, Liam clapped him on the back and even Scotty said, "Well done, Tim."

"Yes," said Seb. "You're proving yourself again, Tim. Not that you needed to. If you hadn't warned me, that could have got nasty."

"That's what I mean," began Liam.

"The thing is," Seb swept on, ignoring the

interruption, "they wouldn't go to those lengths over a bit of bad publicity."

"Then what?" Brian was curious.

"There must be something else on that deck – something they're desperately trying to hide."

"What the hell could that be?" Harold was totally bewildered. He got up impatiently and went back to the bridge.

"Something in those barrels?" asked Tim.

"Barrels?" Liam was instantly alert.

"They were ranged all up one side. I assumed they must be full of whale oil or something."

"So they might be," put in Brian.

"Or something else," said Seb sharply.

"Wait a minute." Liam looked thoughtful. "I suppose –"

"Well?"

"There've been rumours going round for a long time in the Falklands that an Argentine faction is paying someone to pollute the beaches, stir up as much trouble as possible. We've had oil spillages off the coast, seals coated in the stuff; it's been a nagging kind of nuisance." He paused and then warmed to his theme. "Theoretically, nothing could be easier than pouring oil off a catcher; they wouldn't be suspect."

"But what would be the object?" asked Seb. "Could they do it in enough quantity to create a real problem?"

"If they were quick, yes, they could tip a good few barrels over the side. Or maybe shove it in a tank in the hold and use a hose to take it over. And the object?

42

Well, for a start there's a load of kelp farming going on – and it's certainly been interfering with that. And while they're messing that up via the catchers, they could use a factory ship for other – storage – purposes."

"What like?" asked Brian curiously.

"Armaments. Bombs. It all seems a bit far-fetched, perhaps. But the factory ships could be useful to have around – particularly if they're in Argentine pay."

"Who actually owns these?" asked Flower.

"The *Maid of the Sea* and her flotilla?" Liam turned to Seb. "Didn't we think it was an American consortium?"

"Could be." Seb grinned at him and to his relief, Tim could see that the old harmony had been restored, more or less.

"In any case, one way or the other, they can't be very happy about the photography – to say the least."

"So?"

"So in the light of what's happened, shouldn't we get that film ashore? Now?"

Seb nodded. "You're right. I've been so concerned about what they're doing with those poor damned whales, I was getting things out of perspective. You were right about the kids."

There was a howl of protest, after which Flower said, "You're not walking out on us, Dad. We're just as much a part of Green Watch as you."

But just then Harold put his head round the door.

"There's something coming up on the radar, Liam."

"Yes?"

"I think it's a catcher."

"Where's she heading?"

"For us. Again."

Flower gave a startled little cry. Then she looked away, out through the porthole at the grey-green swell.

"Can we outrun her? If we move now?" asked Seb urgently.

Liam shook his head. "In this tub? Not a chance in hell.

Nevertheless *Sea Serpent* was soon speeding back towards the Falklands. It was a cold, bright day, and there was a wintry sheen to the tops of the waves which rolled and broke far out towards the horizon. Tim, Flower and Brian stood in the stern with Harold and watched the *Fortune of War* emerging from what had been no more than an insubstantial smudge behind them. It was depressingly clear that she was gaining fast.

"Are we flat out?" asked Brian helplessly.

Harold nodded. "You bet we are."

"She wouldn't ram us, would she?" asked Tim.

He shook his head. "No chance."

"Then what are they doing?" shrilled Flower.

"Whaling, as usual."

"I didn't see any whales. Maybe they're out to catch something a bit bigger." Her voice shook.

"Hang on." Harold put his arm round her.

"Hang on for what?" She shivered.

"It's going to be OK."

"We can't outrun them."

"It'll be all right."

"What do they want?"

"They're whaling. They're not after us."

"They're after the film," said Brian. "That's all." He knew that Harold was treating her like a child and wondered why.

Liam called them all into the wheelhouse when the *Fortune of War* was about a quarter of a mile behind them, and gaining fast.

"I want everyone to put on a life jacket and stand by the rubber dinghies."

"They *are* going to ram us," muttered Flower.

"No," replied Liam. "This is simply a precaution. Nothing more."

"Dad –" She turned to Seb for reassurance, and Tim felt an icy chill spread over his heart.

"Flower?" His voice was soft, caressing.

"They're not going to ram us, are they?"

"I hope not. But we've been through some scrapes together, haven't we?"

"Yes."

"And come out all right?"

"Just."

He grinned. "There's a lot of room for manoeuvre in the word " 'just'."

Suddenly she smiled too.

Chapter Four

Several times, Seb tried to call up the *Fortune of War* on the radio but there was no response from the relentlessly approaching hulk.

"Dad." Flower seemed to have grown a second skin during the last ten minutes, and for the first time on this trip she appeared confident and controlled. It was as if she had buried her fear of the sea somewhere so deep inside her it was no longer reaching her. If only Seb realized the full extent of that fear, thought Tim, he would have been so proud of her.

"Yes?" His voice was tight and strained.

"If they ram us – if we have to take to the rafts – how far is it to South Georgia?"

"Not far. If that does happen – which I very much doubt – I'll give everyone a compass bearing."

Flower paused and Tim knew that she was about to ask her father something important. A silence gathered on the bridge as if everyone instinctively realized that what she was about to say was going to matter very much indeed.

"If they hit us – somebody – you – anybody – might be killed."

"Rubbish."

"No. I think we need to know the compass bearing now. Just in case."

Seb turned to her and, reaching over, kissed her on the cheek. "Forgive me for being such a coward," he said quietly. "Flower's right. I'm just not facing up to all the possibilities – however remote they may be," he added rather defensively. "OK, if we do have to take to the boats you use this compass bearing." He wrote it down in big letters on a pad on the bridge table. "I'll give everyone a compass." He looked out of the window. The *Fortune of War* was very close. "Now."

For some time, she seemed to keep abreast of them. There appeared to be no one on her deck and it was impossible to make out any faces on her bridge.

"Maybe they're just going to monitor us," said Harold from the wheel, but no one really believed him now.

It's only a matter of time, thought Tim. He no longer felt afraid, but there was a spreading numbness inside him. Even the thought of his mother and father produced only a blur of tears in his eyes.

Still the *Fortune of War* ran parallel with them.

"Any more speed?" asked Seb.

47

Liam shook his head. "She's full out and she's never liked that. Can't you feel her shuddering?"

They could feel the slight tremor but this seemed the least of their worries. *Sea Serpent* continued to rattle along and the *Fortune of War*, with silent hostility, kept pace with her. Over twenty minutes passed during which both vessels surged ahead in unison, but on *Sea Serpent*'s bridge the tension was mounting with every minute. Tim could feel the sweat pouring down from his forehead into his eyes, and when he glanced round at the others, he saw they were dealing with their own fear in a variety of ways. Seb was staring straight ahead, as was Liam, whose fingers were drumming a silent rhythm on the chart table. Harold, behind the wheel, was whistling noiselessly. Scotty strode up and down with a soft, agitated tread. Flower was outwardly calm, her eyes fixed on the heaving waves, and Brian was characteristically reading a book. But he kept looking up and once he whispered, "Come on then, come on."

Tim had almost switched off to the danger. Seb had been taking photographs of the *Fortune of War*'s position, which had still not changed. Maybe she was going to accompany them all the way back to the Falklands. Yes, that was it. A surge of hope swept through him. She was seeing them off, that was all. She was just seeing them off. Eagerly Tim turned to Flower. "You know what?"

"What?"

"She's just taking us back – seeing us off." He was

addressing everybody now. "She's not going to *do* anything – just escort us back to Port Stanley."

Brian put down his book. "Maybe you've got something there. Has he, Dad?"

"I don't know." Seb wouldn't be drawn. But Liam was prepared to join in Tim's optimism. "She certainly isn't doing anything right now."

Instantly Harold and Scotty looked more cheerful. "Guess we got more than a chance now," laughed Harold.

But Flower remained as non-committal as her father. She simply shrugged her shoulders and said, "Keep watching her."

They did, and at least another ten minutes passed.

"Shall I go and make some tea?" Tim suggested.

"Don't leave the bridge," snapped Seb.

"But –"

"I *said* don't leave the bridge."

"Oh, I don't know," interrupted Liam. "I would have thought a cup of tea and a bite to eat might –"

At that moment, the *Fortune of War* changed course and began rapidly veering towards them.

"She's going to hit us," said Seb.

"Should we – let's get out – out on deck," yelled Harold.

"No," Seb insisted. "Stay here."

"I'm –"

"Stay *here*."

The bow of the *Fortune of War* was travelling towards them at a very alarming speed and a great blade of grey-green waves was building up between them.

"Brace yourselves." Seb's voice was very gentle, calmly reassuring. "Hang on to something, and brace yourselves."

Even at the last moment, Tim was still convinced that they were not going to be hit. She was just trying to frighten them, that was all, he kept repeating to himself. Then with a roaring cacophony of sound the *Fortune of War* tore into the *Sea Serpent* midships.

The impact was incredible, and there was a sucking, rending sensation as the *Fortune of War* pulled away. From where he was standing, amidst flying objects and glass, Tim could see the *Fortune of War*'s bows. They were hardly damaged at all, so maybe she hadn't meant to do them any real harm. Perhaps there still a chance that she was merely warning them. But he knew he was being absurdly hopeful. Would she strike again, he wondered. And go on striking until they all plunged to their deaths in the great freezing ocean? But she looked as if she was moving away – steadily moving away. As she did so, the ragged fear hit Tim for the first time, grinding and worming its way into the very heart of his being.

"Brian."

Tim mouthed the name, making only a little indistinct sound. For Brian was lying on the floor, his face covered in blood. The others were standing on the bridge with its shattered windows, staring down at him, seemingly unable to move.

"Brian."

Then the *Sea Serpent* gave a terrible, sickening lurch.

"Get him out," yelled Seb. "Help me get him out on the deck."

The ship was definitely listing now and there was a roar of steam from somewhere in its bowels.

Between them, Liam and Seb began to carry Brian out of the door that was half hanging off its hinges and down the ladder. The others followed to the badly listing deck.

As Tim clattered down the ladder, he could see the *Fortune of War* still withdrawing. There was no one on deck. "Is she going to have another go?" he asked no one in particular.

Harold replied. "No way. She'll have enough explaining to do with the damage to her bows."

"What about Brian?"

Seb looked up. "He'll be OK. He's coming round now. Cut his head but it's not too deep."

As if to remind them of her pain, the *Sea Serpent* gave another lurch and the list dramatically increased.

"Get the life rafts out," yelled Liam and Scotty hastened to obey while Harold sent out a May Day signal.

"Let's have me, Flower, Scotty in one, and Tim, Seb, Brian and Harold in the other," shouted Liam as the *Sea Serpent* gave her third and most shuddering lurch. "She hasn't got long to go."

"Wait." Scotty tried to prise the raft from the buckled railings. "This one's had it."

"So we're all in one raft." Seb stared at Liam. "Will that work?"

"It'll have to. They take six. Now we'll try seven."

There was another lurch, and something in the ship seemed to sigh. Water was only a few metres from the deck now and the list was increasing every minute.

The remaining life raft seemed to be intact and as it inflated itself, Tim could see that it was actually quite large and fortunately had a hood.

"There're water and rations inside," said Harold.

"OK." Liam smiled reassuringly at them. "Prepare to abandon ship."

The raft slid into the water as it lapped round the decking. *Sea Serpent* was at a forty-five-degree angle now and *Fortune of War* was half a mile away.

"Paddle like mad," Seb began. "We don't want to get caught up when she goes down."

Without thinking they grabbed paddles and paddled furiously until the raft was about a hundred yards from the ship. Then, bouncing over the crests, they had a brief glimpse of the *Sea Serpent* turning over on her belly, her prop and screws sticking pathetically out of the water.

As they plunged into a trough, Liam's eyes were full of tears. "Never realized how attached I'd got to the old girl."

When the raft came up on the next crest, there was no sign of *Sea Serpent* at all.

"Brian?"

"I'm OK – bit of a headache. What happened?"

"They got us." Seb stroked his blood-matted hair.

"Everyone OK?"

"Yes."

"Where're we going?"

"South Georgia."

"How long?"

"Twelve hours. Maybe more."

But the next problem was the outboard motor. It took about twenty minutes to start and then ran stickily, as if trying to push its way through treacle.

"Nice equipment," Seb rasped sarcastically to Liam. "Well up to safety regs."

"Can't understand it. That engine was serviced before we sailed from Port Stanley."

"Cowboy," muttered Seb as the engine ran miserably, fitfully on.

"How are you feeling, Brian?" asked Flower, looking down at him in concern.

"I'm OK – bit of a headache." But he was shivering. They were all wearing life jackets and fleece-lined protective clothing, but it was still pretty cold. Brian seemed to be more than just cold, though. He was shivering uncontrollably.

"Dad, take a look at Brian." There was a tremor in Flower's voice.

Seb wormed his way through the overcrowded raft to Brian's side. "OK, old son?"

"Just a headache," he repeated.

"Cold?"

"I'm boiling."

"You've got a bit of a fever – something to do with the knock on your head."

"I'm thirsty, Dad."

"I'll get you some water."

The sea was running fast but the ferocity of the waves was lessening.

"Seb?"

"Yes, Tim?"

"How can they get away with it? I mean, won't someone ask why the *Fortune of War*'s bows are damaged?"

"I expect they've logged it already. Hit something in the fog, but couldn't identify it although they stayed around the spot."

"There wasn't any fog."

"It's patchy," said Liam, staring out into the gathering night. "No one could prove anything either way."

"So they'll get away with it, Liam?" asked Tim, the hot anger crowding his thoughts.

"Very likely. They'll say whatever they ran down was sailing without lights."

"But won't they have to report it?"

"Oh yes – they'll give the wrong position." He sounded very cynical.

"You mean they'll be searching for us in the wrong place?"

"Absolutely. They're obviously counting on our not being picked up."

They were silent. The moon came up over them, pale and wan amidst scudding clouds.

I'll have a lot to tell Mum and Dad, reflected Tim and tried to comfort himself with the thought. He watched the waves through the perspex window of the hood; they were black, scored sometimes by thin moonlight. Brian began to groan and Seb went to him again.

"I'm so hot, Dad."

"It's just the fever."

"And I saw a black castle in the sea."

"Did you?"

"It was on an island, with great big towers and a drawbridge."

"It was only a dream."

"I can see it now."

"It's a dream."

"There are things flying out."

"Things?" Brian sounded so convincing that for a moment Seb thought he really could see something.

"Birds. Birds of prey. They've got rats' heads."

"It's a dream, Brian," he said soothingly.

But Brian began to get more and more excited. "Look, they're sitting on the waves. They're making horrible sounds. They're eating things. Dead sailors. Chewing their heads. And there's music coming from the castle windows. Someone's playing the organ."

Brian raved on for some time until he gradually fell into a deep sleep.

"Will he be better soon?" asked Tim. He looked at Flower but she was staring into the water again. Tim felt a surge of admiration for her. Only he seemed to know the extent of her fear and understand how well she was coping with it.

"He's wrapped in lots of blankets," said Seb. "He'll sweat it out. And by the way, Flower –"

"Yes, Dad?"

"How are you feeling?"

"What do you mean?" she said defensively.

"The water. Is it still your enemy?"

"I don't know what you're on about."

"I think you do."

So he *did* know. Tim was shocked. Seb had known all along. So why hadn't he done anything? Why hadn't he comforted her? And why was he challenging her now?

"Dad –"

"It's OK, Flower. It helps us all if we know what we're afraid of. Scotty, Harold, Liam, Brian, Tim – even me."

"It's only the water."

"Only?" His voice was gentle.

"It seems so weak. We've done so many things, but the water –"

"If you *knew*," snapped Tim, turning to Seb, "why didn't you say?"

"If I had you'd have felt worse, Flower, wouldn't you? If you'd confided in me that would have made it real. As it is, you battled it out for yourself – and looked inside yourself – and won."

"I'm still afraid," she said.

"But you have it under control."

She was silent.

Tim could see what he meant, but it seemed an incredibly hard approach. They all sat quietly for what seemed like hours while Brian still slept. But his breathing was heavy and occasionally he gave a strange, deep snore. Tim could see that Seb was very worried about him.

"I sent off a May Day signal," said Harold. "Why the hell isn't anyone coming?"

"They may well have had the capacity to jam our radio," said Liam. "I've been thinking about that. It's the kind of capacity they would have needed – in case anyone tried to report back that they were fishing in forbidden waters."

"Another thing," put in Scotty. "Have we still got the film?"

Seb patted his protective clothing. "Safely stored away."

"Why didn't they come for it then?"

"Because they would have had to board us, and risk one hell of a fight. I have the feeling they thought they would just ram us, and then see what happened."

"You mean, they know we survived?"

"I've no doubt they saw us launching the raft. They were observing us, of *course* they were."

"I see." Liam obviously hadn't thought of this before. "So what does that mean?"

"It means that when it's daylight they may come for us."

"Run us down *again*?" asked Flower steadily.

"It's possible."

"But that's – we wouldn't stand a chance."

"Well, we could reach South Georgia by dawn."

"And then?"

"We'd at least be on land."

"Is South Georgia inhabited?" asked Tim.

"No," he said flatly.

"So they could come for us there? On the island?"

Seb nodded. "They could," he said.

Chapter Five

Towards dawn, Tim drifted into a fitful sleep. He dreamt of the *Fortune of War*, standing somewhere out at sea, watching them – waiting to run them down again. She was a dark shape in a black sea. Watching. Waiting.

He woke to a slate-grey sky and a lone gull that flew low above them. Tim's eyes darted around the horizon but there was no sign of the *Fortune of War*. Instead there was a landfall in front of them, mountainous, snow-peaked cliffs curving round a bay. Everything was still; even the sea was much calmer.

Seb was up in the bow of the raft, a calm, expectant expression on his unshaven face. The others were huddled together asleep. Tim struggled to his feet and picked his way over the recumbent bodies to join him.

"Seb."

"Sleep?"

"A bit. Are we there?"

"Almost."

"So we're safe?"

"Safer than we were." He grinned but Tim could see the total exhaustion in his eyes.

"How's Brian?"

"Better. Sleeping more peacefully and his temperature's down."

"Did *you* get any sleep?"

"Not a lot. I catnapped."

They both gazed at the approaching shore.

"So the outboard stood up," commented Tim.

"Just about. I had to nurse it through the night. Liam helped. I practically had to force him to go to bed."

"What's it like? South Georgia?"

"Plenty of seals. Volcanic rock. A rather creepy old whaling station. But there's an observatory the other side."

"Inhabited?"

"Not at this time of year. But there'll be a radio. And they leave it open for emergencies."

"So we'll be rescued?"

"Take a few hours to get a chopper out. But yes."

"What about Captain Stanton?"

"He could be there before us," said Seb quietly. "But I'm damned if I'll give up this film."

"He must need it desperately to have attacked us like that."

"Yes, that's what makes me certain that whatever he's got in those barrels – and in anything else on deck – he wants to keep a pretty low profile. And if those pictures appear in the press . . ."

"But nobody's going to recognize what they are," protested Tim.

"The general public, no. The editor, no. But a scientist . . . and you can bet I'll write some pretty riveting copy to go with them. So, we've got to survive on South Georgia until we're picked up. But we'll have to find somewhere dry and comparatively warm for Brian's sake."

"What about the film?"

"I shall have to hide it."

"But where?"

"I know that old whaling station; I've been here several times before. I'll find somewhere."

"Suppose they –"

"Start pulling out my fingernails? I'll just have to think of the whales." He laughed, to turn what he had said into a joke. But Tim knew that if it came to it, he meant it.

Two hours later, the raft had nudged into the inlet.

"It's a long narrow island," a sleepy Liam told them. "About a hundred miles long and twenty miles across. But it's mainly made up of a chain of mountains with glacier-filled valleys. Look, you can see one of them stretching down to meet the sea."

They could: a long silver line in the grey light of a damp, overcast morning. A wind howled through what appeared to be a cluster of ruined buildings on the quayside. The ground around them looked matted with tussock grass that grew right down to the seashore. Moss and lichen covered the jetty while lower down, on its legs, floated a mass of seaweed and kelp. Tim thought it was the most desolate place he had ever seen.

"Captain Cook came here," said Seb, "on his second voyage in search of Antarctica, and he claimed it for the British Crown."

"Yes," said Harold shivering. "Now what did he say about it? Oh, yes, 'Lands doomed by Nature to perpetual frigidness'. I'll never forget that line."

"And where 'not a tree was to be seen, not a shrub even high enough to make a toothpick'," quoted Seb.

"Sounds great," said Brian, sitting up stiffly.

The high, ruined sheds of the old whaling station were a sombre backdrop to the fire that they eventually managed to get going beside the jetty. There was plenty of driftwood, and strange white shapes littered the broken ramp that led to the sheds.

"What are they?" asked Tim.

"Whalebones," replied Harold. "The whole place closed down years ago. It's all done from factory ships now. These old buildings were to do with open boats and hand-thrown harpoons."

They heated up some dried meat, which they ate with hard biscuits, and brewed tea in a dirty old saucepan Flower found in one of the ruined sheds. Then, when they had finished, Seb got up. "I'm going to try and make radio contact. I want everyone else to stay here. I'll be back soon."

"Let me come." Flower was on her feet.

"No." Seb was firm. "I shan't be more than an hour and there's no point in everyone wearing themselves out."

"The film," began Tim.

Seb smiled. "I've already hidden that – and it's probably best that no one knows where it is." He strolled casually away. "See you soon," he said and waved.

"It's been two hours now," said Flower. "What's he doing?"

"No point speculating," said Liam. "Just be patient."

She was, for as long as she could be. It was one o'clock and the wind that had been howling in the high ruined roofs had now turned and was blowing straight in their faces, fanning the smoke from their fire all over them. But, despite the conditions, they stayed where they were until another hour had passed. At which point Flower stood up suddenly. "I'm going after him."

"No." Liam was grimly determined. "Sit down. He'll be back."

"He's in danger."

"He's fine."

"How the hell do *you* know?" Flower rapped out scornfully.

"Because I know him well enough to know he can look after himself."

"And I know him better because he's my father."

They were glaring at each other furiously.

"I'm going," she shouted.

He stood up. "You're staying. Don't push me, Flower."

"I'll push you off this bloody island!"

"Liam –" Brian was sitting up. His voice was urgent.

"You keep out of it."

"Liam –"

"I said, keep *out* of it."

"Don't speak to my brother like that."

"For God's sake!" Brian's voice was hoarse. "Shut up, both of you."

"Take it quietly," said Scotty. "I can see someone. There's someone at the back of the gutting shed, maybe more than one person."

"There *is*," said Harold. "They're watching us."

Liam sat down quickly, signalling Flower to join him.

"What do we do?" asked Tim.

"Keep talking. I'm going up there." Liam lay down as if to sleep and then began to slide towards an old petrol drum. "I'm out of their sightline," he whispered.

"What are you going to do?" hissed Tim.

"Shut up and keep talking," was the reply.

But Liam was not to move far.

"Stop!" The disembodied voice echoed from the huge rusting shed. "Don't move."

Liam froze. "Get back to where you were. Now." Liam didn't move. "If you don't go back, I'll shoot somebody."

Defeated, Liam returned to the fire. They all looked up towards the shed but there was still no one to be seen. Then a man suddenly emerged carrying a small automatic pistol, and followed by three other men.

"Stay where you are, all of you," he barked.

"What does this mean?" asked Liam. "Who the hell are you?"

"I think you know," said the stranger curtly. "I'm Captain Stanton. And I want that film. Now, where is it?"

"We don't know," said Flower. "We really *don't* know."

"Very well. Let me explain the position. As I'm sure you've already guessed, when you sneaked on to my ship, and took your photographs, there was something important on deck. Something we'd much rather you *hadn't* photographed. It would be very unfortunate if the press were to see it."

"*Just* the press?" asked Harold. "First of all you sink our boat and then you threaten us with a gun – just because of a bit of bad publicity? What *was* on deck?"

But Stanton ignored him. Clearly he had no intention of elaborating. "The film," he said. "I want the film."

"We have no idea where it is," said Scotty ponderously.

"Either tell me," shouted Stanton, his temper fraying, "or I'll kill one of the children."

"So it's that important," breathed Brian.

"I'll give you ten seconds." His finger trembled on the trigger and the men behind him watched intently. His nerves were obviously screaming, but Tim knew that however nervous Stanton was he definitely meant business. He raised his arm to take aim.

"Wait," Liam barked.

"Well?"

"The only person who knows where the film is is Seb Howard."

"So where is he?"

"He went off to try and make radio contact."

"We've searched the observatory."

"That's where he was heading."

"You bastard!" Flower suddenly flung herself at Liam, and Harold had to pull her off him, kicking and struggling.

"When you've finished your little civil war . . ." said Stanton with heavy irony. "All right, we'll check again. André, Brett, keep an eye on this lot. Bario, you come with me."

He turned his back on them and walked away while the man called André pulled out his own gun and sat down, calmly covering them. "Might as well make ourselves comfortable," he said. "We may have a long wait."

They sat in silence for the next hour. The light faded, and with it Tim's hopes. He had never felt so desperate or so afraid. Then he noticed a change come over Scotty. He was very tense, very concentrated. Suddenly he stood up.

"Sit down," snapped André.

But instead of obeying, Scotty started walking slowly and deliberately towards him.

"Sit *down*!"

He came on.

"I told you, sit down." André's voice was high, panicky. Still Scotty came on.

"Give it to him," said Brett carelessly. But André was clearly not up to it.

"Stay where you are." The hand that held the gun was shaking.

Scotty suddenly plunged forward, fists and boots flying.

"Now," said Flower. "Now."

She was on her feet and running. Tim got up and started to follow her.

"Brian," she yelled. "Run for it."

"I'm not fit enough. I'll stay here," he said calmly.

Flower stood rooted to the spot in an agony of indecision, while Scotty and André struggled for the gun and Harold and Liam leapt towards them.

"Brian –"

"Go, Flower. Go!"

"No."

"Go!"

Picking up a piece of driftwood, Brett felled Liam

to the ground but Harold grabbed him from behind while Scotty continued to struggle with André.

"Run!" said Tim. "Just run."

Reluctantly she obeyed and together they ran pell-mell over the tussocky grass towards the mountains. As they ran, a shot rang out and when Tim turned he saw Scotty staggering back. But this time it was Flower's turn to shout, "Keep running."

Chapter Six

They ran as fast as they could over the slowly rising ground. Tim's thoughts churned painfully as he forged on. Was Scotty dead? Shouldn't they go back? Where were they going anyway? Finally he had to look back. The old whaling station was out of sight but there was a figure about a hundred yards behind them – a figure that was gaining steadily.

"It's Brett. He's catching up," Tim panted.

"Run harder," said Flower, and somehow she increased the pace.

For a while Tim didn't dare look back again but pounded on, his chest heaving. At last he glanced over his shoulder.

"He's gone."

"Really?"

Tim checked again. "Yes, disappeared."

"Don't – slow – down."

"I'm not. But where – we – going?"

"Into – the – mountains."

"It'll – be – cold –"

"But safe. Now – shut up – talking."

They ran on and on. Eventually Tim got his second wind. In fact he felt terrific as he ran alongside Flower in what were now easy loping strides. He sensed that she, too, was finding her second wind, and as they began to climb sharply it was as if they were running on air and there was no weight in his legs at all.

"Tim."

"Yes?"

"Is that a cave?"

It was up ahead of them, on a bend in the steep mountain path – a path that was gradually petering out. And yes, it was a cave all right, one that went right back into the rock. They reached it and went inside. It smelt of mould and lichen but was oddly comforting. And at least it was out of the chilly wind. They sat down on some boulders deep inside and contemplated what to do next.

"Do you think Scotty's dead?" Tim asked, desperately hoping for reassurance.

She shrugged. "Useless speculating."

"What are we going to do?"

"Find Dad."

"Up here?"

"I thought he'd head for the mountains."

"What about the radio?"

"Let's hope he made contact, that's all. He must have seen them coming, and stayed away."

"Do you think he's going to try and jump them at night?"

"I don't know. But he wouldn't just leave us to it."

"But what are *we* doing?"

"Hiding, for the moment."

"And then?"

"We'll find him. At dawn." Her voice was low and despondent and Tim put his arm round her. "Of course we'll find him."

"I mean, maybe he'll have gone back to the whaling station and got the better of those men, and laid some sort of trap for Stanton and the other guy." She spoke very quickly, the words tumbling out over each other.

Tim agonized for her. She made Seb sound like Superman. "Yes, I'm sure that's right," he agreed encouragingly.

"You don't think so?" Her voice was sharp and angry.

"Of course I do."

"Then you're a fool! Because I don't. Stanton's got that gun. I'm so worried. I'm so afraid for Dad." Her voice broke and Tim gripped her tighter. "It'll be all right."

They were both silent for a while. And then Tim heard a shuffling somewhere in the darkness behind them.

"What's that?" he asked.

"What?"

"Shush. Keep quiet a moment."

"Why?"

"There's something at the back of the cave."

"*Thing?*"

"An animal."

"You're right. There *is* something."

"What do they have here? Anything dangerous? Bears?" Tim asked faintly.

"I can't remember."

They sat in silence, listening for further sounds. Then they went rigid: it was more than a light movement they were hearing now; it was a heavy shuffle.

Tim stood up. "Let's get out."

"Hang on."

"What for?"

"Don't rush. If we run, whatever it is may attack us." She rose quietly to her feet. "Just walk slowly out."

They walked one step at a time towards the mouth of the cave. It seemed to take an eternity, and they were only halfway there when the shuffling suddenly sounded much closer.

"Who's there?" It was a woman's voice.

"Who are you?" Flower whispered.

"Who are *you*?" The voice was brisk, rather matter of fact. Then a torch flashed on. It was powerful and illuminated the whole cave. The woman holding it was young, with dark hair and a weather-beaten face; she was wearing a heavy coat, cords and boots.

"Someone's trying to kill us."

"What on earth are you talking about? You gave me a terrible shock. And of all people to find on South Georgia, two English kids! What are you doing? Are you on your own? Don't you know you could die out here? Have you any idea what temperature it goes down to at night?"

"No," said Flower. "But I can guess."

"You must be *with* someone."

"Our father."

"And who is he? Leaving you alone like this."

"Seb Howard."

"Of Green Watch?"

"Yes."

"My God."

"Are you surprised?" Flower sounded hostile.

"Well, I know he's been around here. You're – you're his daughter?"

"Yes."

"I've heard a lot about you."

"This is Tim, my cousin. He's another member of Green Watch."

"What happened? Where's Seb? Is he OK?"

"No," said Flower, her whole body shaking now.

"Is he hurt?"

"We're looking for him." Her voice broke.

"I see. Well, you'd better come in and get warm. And tell me all about it."

"Come *in*?" asked Tim incredulously.

"Yes, this is my home. At least it's the front door. Come in and tell me what's happened, and if there's

73

anything we can do, well, we'll do it."

Tim breathed a sigh of relief.

"Come this way. My name's June – June Rose." She led them to the back of the cave, where they squeezed through a small opening and continued down a narrow corridor in the rock. "It's not far," she said.

The corridor began to broaden out and with a shock they suddenly found themselves in a small cave furnished with a wooden table and chairs, a bunk, a bookcase and a calor gas stove. It was warm and cosy. But the most startling thing of all was that the walls were completely covered with pictures of whales.

"I've got a bit of thing about them," she said, seeing them staring. "Soup?"

They nodded, and while June Rose was preparing the soup she said again, "Tell me all about it."

Flower told her the whole story, from the moment they had first boarded the doomed *Sea Serpent* until the moment they lost their pursuer on the mountainside. When she had finished June served out the soup in silence.

"That all makes a lot of sense," she said at last. "I'm a naturalist, here on a project for the Wildlife Fund, studying birds and keeping an eye on the whales. No one will do a damn thing about those whales."

"What do you think was on the deck of that factory ship?" asked Tim. "That they're so frightened will appear in the press?"

"I don't know, but it'll be a damn sight more

important than barrels of oil for chucking over the side and polluting the Falkland beaches. The question is what – and the other question is, where's your dad?" she said, turning to Flower. "Maybe I know."

"Where?" Flower's voice was eager.

"If he is hiding out – plotting his next move – he could be in the Sea House."

"What on earth's that?"

"He used it once. To birdwatch with me. It's a big cave, just above the waterline." She looked at her watch. "It gets flooded by the tide, or rather most of it does. There's a ledge where you can shelter, but the tide should be out now in any case."

"Do you think he could be there?"

"It's the only place I can think of. I hope he is, but either way I'm afraid he *won't* have made radio contact."

"Why not?" asked Tim anxiously.

"Because the radio's out of action."

"Broken?"

"Broken down."

"Can we go out to the Sea House now?" demanded Flower.

"No more soup?"

"Please can we hurry!"

"OK. It's a bit of a way. But, incidentally, don't worry about him too much. Your father's a very resourceful man."

"I know he is," replied Flower proudly.

It took them about half an hour to reach the cave. They climbed back down the mountain, scrambling over precipitous rocks and mounds of tussock grass in the direction of the sea. Darkness had fallen and a bright moon was shining. "We're very much in silhouette against the landscape in this light," said June. "But that's a risk we're going to have to take." She pressed on in front of them, a slight figure who had no difficulty coping with the uneven terrain. Eventually they arrived at a rocky shelf overlooking the glistening sea.

"It's a bit of a scramble down," she said. "Watch your step."

It certainly was, but the moonlight picked out the tumbled rocks and it was easy to see where they were putting their feet.

"It's here."

A narrow entrance yawned in front of them, and below the sea grumbled restlessly at the rocky fore-shore.

"We go down inside now."

"Shouldn't we call for him?" asked Flower.

June shook her head. "No, we don't know where Stanton and his mates are; the last thing we want to do is draw attention to ourselves. Just follow me."

She was briskly commanding and they followed her meekly through the narrow entrance and down an equally narrow incline. It was a long way down, but eventually they arrived in a large cave smelling strongly of the sea. The pounding of waves was very close.

"He's not here," said Flower in a hopeless voice.

"I wouldn't expect him to be."

"What on earth do you mean?" Tim said accusingly.

"There's an inner cave. Hang on."

She took hold of a section of rock and tugged. It looked immovable but suddenly it slid aside.

"Dad –" Flower bounded in and Tim followed. But this cave was empty too.

"Where is he?"

June Rose laughed. They had not heard her laugh before and it was an unpleasant, uncontrolled sound.

"Where is he?" Flower repeated.

Tim felt uneasy. Something was horribly wrong.

"Your dad?"

"Yes, who else?"

"I hope he's dead."

"What?" Flower was aghast.

"I hope he's dead." She laughed again, and it was the same uncontrolled sound.

She's potty, thought Tim suddenly. She's crazy.

"I don't understand." Flower stared up at June Rose in amazement.

"The sliding door? We made that."

"We?"

"Ken Stanton and I."

"Stanton – Stanton and you?" Tim felt completely shattered.

"Very much so. I'm going to marry him."

"Where's my dad?" asked Flower ferociously.

"I haven't the faintest idea."

"Then why are we here?"

"Why do you think?"

They shook their heads, uncomprehending.

"Because I'm going to kill you," she shouted.

"Kill us?" whispered Tim.

"I want to help Ken, you see. I always want to help Ken."

"But why?"

"Because of the whales."

"I still don't –"

"The bloody whales. They killed my family. Years ago now. But I can remember every detail."

"What happened?" He wanted to keep her talking – and he knew she wanted to talk. Flower was just standing beside him. Watching her. Waiting.

"We were out there – out there off the island. There was a whale but we were well out of the way." There was a glazed, far-away look in her eyes as she spoke. "There were a lot of whales, all running before the ship. They hit us. My husband drowned, my two children . . . They all drowned."

"I'm sorry," whispered Flower.

"But it wasn't the whales' fault," said Tim. "They were afraid."

"They drowned them all. I tried to save them. They found me on the shoreline. I was wearing a wet suit but my hands . . ." They hadn't noticed before but when she held them up now, they saw that one hand had three fingers missing. "I was in hospital for a long time. Then I came back. Came back here."

"Why?" asked Tim.

"To kill the whales of course."

"Kill the whales? How could you possibly do that?"

"I'm a scientist. I invented something that Ken Stanton's got now. It's a harpoon with a poisoned tip. Once it goes in, the whale's dead in seconds. It would have been on the deck. I know Ken was deciding whether or not to give the harpoon some unofficial tests. The problem is that it could be banned by the International Whaling Commission. If they knew about it, that is. But if Stanton can use it, it's going to speed up catching enormously." She laughed wickedly, like a delighted child.

"Let us go," said Tim. "You don't want to hurt us."

"I do. You're part of them – part of the whales."

"Don't be so stupid," Flower began and then realized that she wasn't listening. She was looking towards the sea, which by now, was trickling in at the mouth of the cave.

"The tide's coming in," muttered Tim. "Coming in fast." And with that he launched himself at June Rose. Seconds later, to his amazement, he found himself lying flat on his back on the rock.

"Don't try it again," she said quietly. "I'm a black belt in karate."

"What are you going to do?" asked Flower evenly.

"I'm going to leave you here."

"The tide's coming in," yelled Tim again.

"Yes, and it fills the cave to the ceiling. But the

79

cold will kill you before you drown." She smiled.

"You can't do that!"

"No?"

"Listen," said Flower. "Let's talk about the whales – let's talk about them now."

"No."

"I think we should."

"What's the point?"

"You're all – all messed up. It was an accident. They didn't kill your children deliberately."

"You go to the whales. If that's what you want."

"Please –"

"Go to them." And she began sliding back the rock.

Chapter Seven

"How long?"

"Before it comes in? It is now."

"Could we swim?" Tim asked.

"This is the Antarctic – almost. We'd be dead in a few seconds."

"Try the rock again."

"No chance. It opens from the outside."

"What the hell are we going to do?" Tim was getting frantic.

"Think."

"*Think?*"

"There must be a way."

"Climb," he said suddenly. "She said there was a ledge." His voice was eager.

"There's no ledge. I've looked."

"And the walls are smooth."

More water splashed in.

"I've looked carefully. There isn't anything, not even the famous ledge," repeated Flower in a whisper. A spate of icy water ran over the floor of the cave. "We're going to be sucked down." The whisper was hoarser now and Tim could see that her phobia had surfaced and squeezed everything else out of her mind.

"We're going to get out," he said with quiet authority.

"How?"

"I don't know yet, but we're going to." He scanned the cave walls once more in desperation and then went out to the stone slab and tried repeatedly to move it. But it wouldn't budge. What the hell was he going to do? The trickle of water had risen by at least an inch and was threatening to cover his shoes. Then, looking up at the craggy roof, he saw a very slim possibility. But at least it *was* a possibility.

"Look."

Flower's whole body seemed to have stiffened and she looked up with real physical difficulty.

"What's there?" Her voice was expressionless.

"A funnel, or something."

"A way out?" But she sounded hopeless, almost resigned.

"Give me a hand up. I'll try it."

Flower did as she was told, moving like an automaton, and Tim, standing on her shoulders now, managed to get some purchase on the rock face. He

pulled himself towards it and reached out for a hand-
and a foothold. A vivid memory of how terrified he
had been when Seb took him rock climbing in
England flashed through his mind, and of how
humiliated he had felt afterwards. But he had no time
for doubts now; all he could do was to take a gigantic
risk. Somehow Tim's fingers found niches in the
rock, and with a grinding effort he succeeded in
pulling himself up against it.

"Got it."

"The water – it's rising." Flower's voice was very
unsteady now.

"We're going to get out," said Tim firmly.

"I know we are," she replied, in an effort to control
her fear. "We're going to be all right."

She's so brave, thought Tim with a rush of
affection and renewed determination, so damn brave!
Then he thought of his parents – of his mother
waiting at home and his father in prison. He pictured
the bad news filtering through to them, and finally
shut his mind to the impossibly painful images.

He climbed up the funnel, hand over hand. There
was a strong smell of seaweed and the roof was damp
and clammy to the touch. Tim realized that, once it
had filled the cave, the water must drive itself up here
too – and if he wasn't quick enough he would be
drowned in the narrow crevice. It was a horrible
thought and he continued climbing as fast as he
could, while the chimney grew ominously narrower.

"OK?' she shouted up.

"Fine."

"Is there a way out?"

"I'm sure there is," said Tim with grim optimism. But the further he climbed, the narrower the chimney became. Gradually the truth began to dawn: there was no way out here.

"What's happening?"

"It's fine."

"Can we get out?"

"Sure."

"The water's over my ankles."

"It'll be OK."

"Tim –"

"Yes?"

"It's not OK, is it?"

"Of course it is."

"Tim –" Her voice was quiet and calm. "It's not OK."

"That's right." He was staring up at a blank rock face. "You're right."

"Come down."

"No, you come up here. Maybe the water doesn't reach this far."

"Is it wet up there?"

"Yes."

"Then it does."

Tim pressed his head against the damp rock, thinking about his parents. This was it then. They were going to die. "There must be a way," he said faintly.

"Come down."

"We could swim out."

"We'd drown."

"There must –"

"Come down," she said sharply.

This time Tim did as he was told. When he reached the floor of the cave he discovered that the water was almost up to his knees. It was very cold.

"She's barmy," he said. "They'll hang her."

"They don't do that nowadays," replied Flower. "And even if they did, it wouldn't do us much good."

"I suppose not. Come on, let's both have a go at that stone."

They pushed and heaved and struggled while the water crept up their thighs.

"God, it's cold."

"My feet are going numb," said Flower. But she was still very calm.

They continued pulling at the stone but it wouldn't budge. It was damp and slimy to the touch and quite unyielding.

"OK," said Tim, looking down at his nails and noting with some surprise that they were chipped and his fingers bleeding, "what now?"

The numbing water was up to their waists. Tim put his arm round Flower, and she did the same to him. Meanwhile, the water kept creeping up.

"It won't be too bad," she whispered.

"No," said Tim miserably.

"I can't feel anything anyway."

"Neither can I."

"What's that?" she said suddenly.

"What?"

"I thought I heard something."

Tim turned and stared at the stone. It was rolling back.

"Tim! Flower!" Seb stood there as the water rushed through the gap into the second cave. At first they just gawped at him, unable to believe their eyes.

"Well, don't just stand there!"

She was the first to react. "Dad?"

"Get moving."

They turned and waded towards him, and Seb gathered them up in his arms whilst the water, lower now that it had more room to flood, surged about them.

"June Rose," said Flower.

He nodded. "She passed me on the mountainside but she didn't see me. She was muttering and looking so crazily gleeful that I followed her. I felt instinctively that something awful had happened."

"Is she barmy?" asked Tim, his teeth chattering in response to the cold and the sudden realization that they were safe. Oh God, they were safe! It was a miracle.

"Yes," said Seb. "She was driven barmy. I've known her for a long time, but she hates me because I protect the whales. Anyway, in the course of her rambling I caught the words 'kids' and 'sea house', so I dashed down here."

"Thank God you did," said Flower. Tears were pouring down her face. "We thought she was nice at first. She seemed so kind and helpful."

"She *was* nice once. But the tragedy completely altered her. She's obsessed now. I thought they'd forced her to leave South Georgia."

"They?" said Tim blankly.

"The authorities. She's been a menace here, smashing equipment and things."

"The radio?"

"That and lots of other equipment. But don't let's hang around. Come and let's get you dried off."

"Where, Dad?"

"Her cave, of course."

"What? Won't she –"

"She's not going to have any choice. You leave that to me."

Flower let out a whoop of joy and brushed away her tears.

"Both run," said Seb. "You'll warm up that way."

They ran – where the ground allowed them to – and it seemed only minutes before they were back at the cave.

"Wait here." Seb raised a finger to his lips. "I'll go in." Without waiting for an answer he hurried inside.

"Will she put up a fight?" whispered Tim. "I mean, she said she was a karate black belt."

"Dad can cope with that. Besides . . ."

"Besides what?"

"I don't think she will. I remember him talking about someone on South Georgia. Someone he wanted to help. That he was fond of."

"Her?"

"Could be. She does need help."

Tim was about to say something when a figure detached itself from the shadows at the mouth of the cave. "She's not there."

"Where's she gone, then?" asked Tim in agitation.

"To Stanton?" Seb's voice was cool. "Let's all go inside. The fire's still lit."

They marched through the outer cave and into the welcoming warmth of the interior.

"I'll stay near the entrance," said Seb. "I've got good ears; I'll hear her coming. And then we'll give her a little surprise. You two, dry yourselves off."

They did as they were told, and while they were sitting round the calor gas fire, their clothes steaming, Flower said, "What's the next move, Dad?"

"Well, we can't stay on the island. That's for sure."

Tim and Flower told him then what had happened down at the jetty. "It was horrible leaving Brian like that but he insisted we should run for it," Flower finished.

"Stanton's not likely to harm them, until they find us," said Seb. "And I've still got the film." He patted his pocket. "Thought it was better to keep it on me in the end. So the next move is to get off the island."

"In the rubber dinghy?" asked Flower incredulously.

"Maybe, unless they've destroyed it – which they will have done if they have any sense."

"Then what could we use?" asked Tim.

"There's an old wooden whaler in one of the sheds. We had it out a couple of summers ago. It floated then."

"And if it doesn't?" Flower's voice was steady and Tim wondered for a moment if the nightmarish events in the cave might have helped her overcome her fear.

"Just off the coast," said Seb, ignoring her, "is a wrecked coaster. It's lying aground on the other side of the island. If we could reach her . . ."

"But what's the use?" Tim was suddenly desperately tired. "It would only be a bit of a holding action. They'd come for us. If they didn't stop us first when we pushed the whaler out."

"The whaler's the risk. If I could get to the coaster, I reckon I could repair the radio."

"The radio?"

"The one I took from the weather station." Seb grinned at the amazed look on their faces. "I've got it in a waterproof in one of the coves. I just need time. More time than I've got on this island."

Flower smiled. "Good old Dad. You weren't a boy scout for nothing, were you?"

"Actually, I was an air scout."

"Never mind that," said Tim impatiently, looking ahead for other dangers. "What about the others? And what about June Rose?"

"We'll wait here till dawn," said Seb. "I expect she'll be back by then. But we'll be ready for her." He sounded reassuringly confident.

But there was no sign of her for hours and gradually their confidence began to ebb. Tim sensed that Flower was becoming increasingly worried about her brother. So was Seb. But he seemed determined to wait until dawn.

"It's a good time," he said. "People are at a major psychological as well as physical disadvantage at dawn. We'll go down to the jetty and see what's happening. Maybe there'll be some prisoners to release . . ." His voice tailed away. "I should never have involved you all in this," he said sadly. "Liam was right. I've exposed you to unnecessary danger quite recklessly. Look what poor demented June tried to do to you! And Brian, who knows what's happened to him?"

"We're grown up," said Flower simply. "We're not kids any longer."

Seb stared at her and then looked away. Tim knew she was right and that Seb had silently acknowledged the fact.

Chapter Eight

Dawn came, and with it lashing rain. They were soaked again, within minutes of leaving the cave. Cautiously making their way down the mountain, they headed back towards the giant whaling shed and the quayside.

The rain wasn't letting up and visibility was reduced to just a few metres. The wet tussock grass kept tripping them up and the mist seemed to be continually closing in. The path led down between large boulders of rock and it was impossible to see round each corner. The three of them grew increasingly tense as they reached beach level.

"No one around." Seb edged forward, flattening himself against the rock. "Stay there." He took a few more steps and then beckoned them on. "Stay together, and come this way round." They were slowly edging around the back of the huge shed. The rain pelted down on the corrugated iron roof, making more than enough din to cover their movements. "Now, wait at the back. If anyone comes, run like hell."

"Can't we –" began Flower.

"Stay." His voice was fierce. After five minutes of agonized waiting, Seb came back to join them.

"No sign of anyone," he said flatly.

"Sure?" Flower was so tense that she could hardly bring the word out.

"Yes, I've looked everywhere."

"Not quite everywhere," said Brian as he sauntered round the other side of the shed.

"What the hell?" Seb stepped back.

Tim stared at Brian, utterly baffled. Where on earth had he sprung from?

"Where are the others?" snapped Seb, relief making him angry. Then he reached forward, gathered Brian into his arms and hugged him.

"You're crushing me," he protested.

Slowly Seb released him.

"They've taken them to the factory ship."

"And how did you get clear?"

"The fight was really horrible," said Brian. "I was still so weak, I couldn't do much. Poor Liam was knocked out almost immediately and Scotty was shot in the arm. They soon got the better of Harold after that."

"Then how did you –"

"I did a bunk while they were tying up Harold and hid out for hours in an old shepherd's hut. Then, some time during the early morning I came back to see what had happened. There was no one here but one of them had managed to scrape a message on the door of one of the smaller sheds. It just said 'TAKEN TO MAID OF –' "

"You OK?" said Flower.

"I'm a bit tired." Brian yawned. "Oh, by the way, I've got a prisoner."

"You what?" Seb gazed at his son in amazement.

"She's in the old kitchen. Tied to a boiler. I gagged her too, actually." Brian yawned again.

"She –" began Tim.

But Flower was too quick for him. "You mean, you caught June Rose?"

"Is that her name? She was with Stanton earlier. He and the other man came back and were cursing André and Brett for going off and stranding them here. Then they put back for him and Stanton tried to persuade her to go too. But she refused. Said she was determined to get you, Dad. She came back here an hour ago. So I jumped her."

"She's a black belt in karate," said Tim wonderingly.

"Is she? Then it's lucky I hit her on the back of the head with that bit of wood."

"It *is* lucky," put in Seb. "I would say you were *very* lucky."

"She went out cold, so I dragged her over to the kitchen and had her tied up before she came round.

She went bananas. So I had to gag her. She was making such a racket."

"And then?" asked Flower.

"I sat and read my book. Till you lot turned up. What have you been doing?"

Briefly they told him and even Brian listened wide-eyed. Then he said, "She seems a bit of a case."

"Let's take a look at her," said Seb briskly. "Stanton and co. could be back any minute. They won't have given up."

They walked over to a group of huddled concrete buildings on the quayside that seemed to have survived intact. One of them was a large and very old-fashioned mass-catering kitchen housing massive stoves and work surfaces, all well preserved but covered in dust. Strapped to the boiler in the corner, her eyes bulging with fury, was June Rose. Seb stepped over and undid her gag. A torrent of vile abuse burst forth, but Seb seemed to know how to handle her.

"Shut up."

The yells subsided into incomprehensible mutters.

"I *said*, shut up, June."

She was silent now, her eyes on him. Tim had expected them to be full of anger but instead they were beseeching. Then she caught sight of Flower and would have burst into renewed abuse had not Seb quickly interrupted her.

"You tried to kill my daughter, and my nephew."

"To hell with them!" Her eyes were blazing now.

"You're totally callous, aren't you? Two kids, and you'd do that to them."

"They deserve all they get."

"But why?"

"They're protecting the whales. So they can take the consequences."

"You'll be taking the consequences. I'm having you arrested."

"Stanton will stop you."

"He won't. For now, we shall have to leave you here, but –"

"Do what the hell you like in the short term," she snarled.

"Meaning?"

"Meaning I'll get you in the end, Seb Howard."

"June –" There was a soft note to his voice.

"Don't pretend you care a jot about me."

"I wanted to help you, June, but you tried to kill my children."

"One of your kids nearly killed me."

"And if you had, I might have killed *you*," he continued, ignoring her retort. "You're a human being with a mind – intelligence."

"What are you driving at, Seb?" she said mockingly.

"I'm trying for the last time to get you to think straight. Those whales didn't kill your family. They haven't the ability to think, to plan. It was a tragic accident."

"So you say. But you're their protector, aren't you?" she sneered.

"They *need* protecting. So many beautiful creatures are becoming extinct because –"

"They're magic. Black magic," she broke in, ignoring him.

"Come on!"

But there was a wild look in her eyes. "They're black magic, Seb. And you're on their side."

"You're – you're not yourself, June. You haven't been for a long time."

"Are you trying to say I'm crazy?" She laughed and Tim shivered. It was the same laugh he had heard in the cave.

"I'm trying to say that you're imagining something that didn't happen."

Her chilling laughter ended in screams of abuse until Seb, unable to take any more, retied the gag. Then he checked the ropes while June Rose stared down at him with the eyes of a malignant witch.

"You did a good job there, Brian."

"I've always prided myself on my knots, Dad."

Flower took her father's arm. "You've tried."

"God knows why, after what happened!"

"You're a good man." Suddenly, to Tim, Flower sounded old enough to be her own father's mother. It was weird.

"She – she wasn't always like this," said Seb. "Before the accident she was a very gentle, intelligent person." He looked into June's mad, burning eyes. "Maybe with treatment . . . Anyway we must get on. Let's go outside and talk." He looked utterly drained.

"Here she is."

The old whaling boat looked enormous. But Seb was confident that they could drag her down to the sea. "Let's hope she'll float, that's all."

He began to explain the plan to Brian. When Seb had finished, he nodded and said, "Only one thing though."

"Yes?"

"What happens if they see us?"

"They'll attack. Probably sink her. And that will be that. We won't have a rubber dinghy this time." He looked up at Brian with a hopeful expression. "Unless . . ."

Brian shook his head. "No, Dad. They slashed her to bits."

"So that's it." Seb turned slowly back to Flower and Tim. "Listen, all three of you. I aim to row the boat down to the cove, pick up the radio and head for the coaster. It's not that far; the whole process could take under an hour. But I have to stress, if we're seen we've had it. So . . ."

"We know the risk, Dad," said Flower quietly.

"Do you?"

"Yes," said Tim and Brian in unison.

"I could row her myself. I don't need any of you to help."

"So?" asked Brian with mock innocence.

"So the three of you could stay here."

"And wait for Stanton?"

"He wouldn't kill you."

"June Rose?" queried Flower. "I think she would,

right away. Don't you, Dad?"

"God." Seb buried his head in his hands. "Liam was –"

"Wrong," said Tim. "We're with you. All the way. Whatever happens. But the others are helpless. What are we going to do about them?"

"Nothing." Seb's face was set and expressionless. "They'll be safe with Stanton – unless he gets hold of the film."

The whaler rolled down the slipway unprotesting and entered the water with a splash. There was a tense moment as they waited for her to fill with water. But she didn't.

"She's OK," yelled Flower. She didn't glance at the sea once.

She *is* cured, thought Tim. She really *is* going to be all right.

"Wait." Seb was more cautious. "Let her settle down."

They waited, but not a drop of water collected inside her timbers.

"All right," said Seb, fitting the oars in the rowlocks. "Let's go."

Tim looked around. Thank God the mist was still with them.

It was like rowing through cotton wool and the splash of the oars was muffled, as if they were densely wrapped in layers of gauze. Now and then Seb motioned to Brian to stop rowing and lifted his own oars out of the water, listening intently. But there was no sound. In what seemed no time at all he had beached the boat in a small, rocky cove and was bundling the radio on board. Then they began rowing again, up the coastline, still pausing to listen for any sound of pursuit. Flower swopped with Brian at the oars, and later Tim with Flower. As he rowed, Tim could hardly bear the tension, expecting any moment, to hear the engines of a surging boat. But there was still no sound.

"There she is."

"Where?"

"Dead ahead."

The coaster was a broken outline, lying halfway up a gently rising shingle beach. It was just before eight am and as the mist began to lift sea and landscape were a uniform grey.

"We'll hide the boat round the other side. There's another cove and I think there are some caves at sea level." Seb sounded very confident now and gradually Tim's tension eased. Perhaps it was going to be all right after all.

The water surrounding the coaster was smooth and the waves simply lapped at the rocks rather than breaking over them. Her name was still faintly to be made out over the bow: *Esperance*.

"She's French. The name means hope – a good sign, I reckon." Seb was jovial.

"Do you think you can mend the radio?" asked Flower.

"June gave it a good bashing, but yes, I reckon I

can. I need time, which we haven't got. But if the *Esperance* will give us sanctuary . . ." They looked up at her rusty, broken bows. Half the railings were trailing off the decking and there was a great hole gouged in her stern. A solitary herring gull sat on her bridge. The rocks around her were sharp and vicious-looking, sticking out of the sea like the warning fingers of a crippled giant.

"How do we get on to her?" asked Tim.

"There's a rope on the other side. Can you climb over?"

"Yes, I think so," he replied doubtfully.

"I'll get you up there. Then I'll beach the whaler in the next cove on and walk back. I can get on to her over the bows. It's a bit of a climb, but I reckon I can make it."

"Be careful, Dad," said Brian. "We don't want an accident out here. Not at this stage."

"And we won't be having one," replied Seb firmly.

Tim looked up at the rope in horror. It seemed very long and the side of the *Esperance* enormously high. There were a few knots in it, but not nearly enough for him to be sure that he could do it. He glanced quickly at Flower and Brian, but they were looking up at the rope as if it was an easy climb in an adventure playground. He wondered again about Flower's fear of the sea. But she was giving nothing away.

"OK." Seb manoeuvred the boat under the rope. This side of the *Esperance* was even more battered,

100

and there was a razor-sharp rock rearing up just beside her. "Tim, do you want to go up first?"

For a moment he sat rigid. Then he slowly rose to his feet.

"Go for it, Tim," said Brian softly. They were all rooting for him, he knew that. Tim grabbed the rope, swung himself clear of the whaler, and began to climb.

"Don't look down," whispered Flower.

Quite suddenly – and unexpectedly – a surge of confidence filled him, as if all the good will from the other members of Green Watch below had given him tremendous power. He climbed with an increasing sense of elation, not looking down, his hands and feet working in rhythm, his knees locked around the rope. Tim felt strong and resourceful – and, above all, confident. He felt another weight on the rope. Someone was just behind him and that was enormously reassuring too. What would his school friends think? Here he was, climbing a rope on to a wrecked ship in the South Atlantic. It was almost too perfect an adventure story – if it hadn't been so terrifyingly real.

Once on deck, Tim looked around him, still glowing with satisfaction from the climb. He felt he could tackle anything now. The *Esperance* was in very poor shape with most of her cowling damaged and her hatches broken and in some cases missing altogether. Looking down one of them all he could see was a dark pit and equally dark water lapping below. He turned back to haul Brian up, and then

Flower. All three stood panting, gazing at the devastation around them.

"She's deteriorated a lot since we were here a couple of years ago," said Brian.

"Let's have a look at the forward cabins." Flower sounded more positive. "They could be OK still."

They were. The blankets and bunks were horribly damp but no rain had got inside.

"There're more down here." Flower clambered down a rickety ladder and they followed her. The cabins here smelt musty but were less damp. They had quite a homely atmosphere and Tim suddenly realized how hungry he was – and that he had not thought about food until now. "We got anything to eat?"

Brian grinned. "I was wondering when you were going to ask that." He patted the pockets of his waterproofs. "I've got a bottle of mineral water and some other stuff – dried meat and pemmican – I nicked out of the raft."

"How did you manage that?"

"I did it when I got back – and before nice Auntie June arrived. They might have smashed up the raft, but Stanton didn't think to take the food."

"Good for you," said Tim.

"So we've got food and shelter. Dad's got the radio and we haven't seen Stanton. Yet. Things could be worse."

They went up to the deck again and walked forward to the prow. Seb was striding up the beach. He waved, walked casually towards the battered prow and – to Tim's astonishment – began to climb up it, using tiny cracks and crannies in the battered steel as hand- and footholds.

"The human spider," said Brian proudly. "I couldn't do that."

"Nor could I," replied Flower. Tim knew he certainly couldn't. But Seb continued to climb, as casually as before and without much apparent effort. Soon they were hauling him over the side of the deck. But Tim knew that he didn't really need their assistance.

"Where did you learn to do that?" he asked incredulously.

Seb grinned. "Self-taught. Like everything else I do."

"But –"

"Anyway, we haven't got the time to go into my climbing abilities." He was unstrapping the radio from his back. "I want to get on with this."

"I'll fix the food," said Brian. "Such as it is."

"We're lucky to have anything at all." Seb was looking at his watch. "I'll go up to what's left of the bridge and start work. We may not have much time."

Chapter Nine

They ate, Seb worked, they watched. But there was no sign of pursuit: the South Atlantic stretched out into seeming infinity, its calm, grey surface unbroken.

As they were sitting in the dank cabin, huddled together for warmth, Flower suddenly said, "Listen."

"I can't hear anything," said Brian.

"Shut up. Keep listening," she insisted.

Tim's nerves tightened. What were they listening for? Then he heard it, very faintly in the bowels of the ship. It was like very faint music.

"Music?" he whispered, bewildered.

"Come on." She was already on her feet and making her own way down the ladder.

"Where're we going?"

"Down."

"But she's flooded."

"Only at a certain level. Come on." Her head disappeared and Brian and Tim began to climb down after her. As they climbed, the faint sound became stronger. It was extraordinary, almost impossible to describe: a kind of heavenly music, soft and alluring, mysterious and somehow, very, very old. Tim was reminded of the singing he had once heard in a cathedral, and yet this was different. Sometimes it sounded a long way away; sometimes it sounded very close indeed.

Flower led them down into the very heart of the ship.

"Where are we?" asked Tim.

"I think it's the mess room," said Flower. There was an old girlie calendar hanging on the wall and a scattering of broken stools and tables. "Put your ear to the wall, and listen."

They both did as she said. As they pressed their ears to the *Esperance*'s damp, cold side, the music instantly became more resonant. It seemed to fill Tim's head with its mournful, yet joyful, extraordinary sound which changed mood and key all the time.

"It's the whales, isn't it?" he said quietly as the realization dawned. "They're singing."

Flower nodded, her eyes sparkling.

The sound swelled and faded. In his mind's eye Tim could see the vast underwater giants, calling, singing to each other. Were they transmitting warnings or greetings? Or was this perhaps the music of love? Then the sound faded out altogether. Tim strained his ears, desperate to hear more. But it had gone.

"Yes," said Flower. "It's fantastic, isn't it?"

"Have you heard it before?"

"Once or twice, when we were here a couple of years ago."

"Brian?"

He nodded. "It's weird. Beautiful."

"Have you – have you heard it on this ship?" Tim asked Flower.

She shook her head. "No, never."

They stood in silence, willing the music to return. But it didn't. Then they heard Seb's voice. "What are you lot doing?"

"Listening to the whales."

He clambered down to join them. "You were lucky."

"It was amazing," said Tim. "Really amazing."

"Yes, and there's a vast range of frequencies."

"What's it for, though?"

"Keeping in contact with their group. Detecting food. A mother singing to her cub . . . Of course water's a much better conductor of sound than air; in fact it travels about five times as far."

"So they're miles away?"

"Probably. But they could be near. One of them might be. Did you notice the song change continuously?"

Tim nodded.

"So, an individual whale might adopt new songs – or a new song – sung by another whale in the area," said Brian.

"And that means," put in Flower, "that the whales are in direct contact."

"It's magic."

Seb grinned at Tim. "Whatever it is, it's one of the best sounds in the world. Just suppose we never heard it again . . ." It was as if Seb had stopped talking to them and was talking to himself now. His eyes had that cold, hard look again.

"How's the radio?" asked Brian as they climbed back on to what remained of the bridge. It was midday.

"I'm winning," said Seb. "At least I think I am."

"How long?" Flower's voice was tense.

"Another couple of hours. I hope."

But Tim, who was staring out over the water, was not listening. "Look!" he shouted.

A spume of water had risen, followed by another. Then he had a fleeting glimpse of a dark, gliding shape.

"It's a whale," he yelled.

They all rushed to the side and saw other spumes, other shapes.

"There're a lot of them," said Seb quietly. "Quite a colony."

As they watched, they saw that there were about half a dozen whales moving gracefully, sometimes diving, sometimes breaking the surface of the water.

They were enormous; swooping giants, the water pouring off their cavorting bodies in great showers. Tim sensed that the whales were somehow protecting them. Perhaps it was fanciful, but they made him feel safe; as if he was in their world now, an old, magical world where the whales were massive talismans guarding them against Stanton, and June Rose, and their like.

"It's a good luck sign," said Flower, echoing his thoughts.

"We're going to need it," replied Seb, his eyes fixed ahead.

"What's up?"

"There's something out there. A ship."

"There can't be. We haven't radioed." Tim's voice was faint.

"Flatten yourselves," Seb yelled. "It's a catcher!"

They lay down on the cold floor of the bridge.

"Are they after the whales, or us?" asked Flower.

"God knows. Brian, see if you can inch your way to that window and tell us what the hell's going on."

Brian slid across to the window. Crouching on all fours, he peered out. "It's a catcher all right. But a different one."

"What's it called?"

"*Song of the South.*"

"Could still be attached to the *Maid.*"

"On the other hand –" Brian kept watching. "She's not going for the whales."

"For us?"

"Difficult to say. She's getting nearer – but – hang on – she's anchoring."

"Keep low."

"I am. Can't see anyone on deck. Oh yes, there's someone on the bridge now. I think they're checking the coast with binoculars. Now they're checking us. Wait, someone's coming out on deck. They've got something – it's a megaphone."

"They must know we're here," said Flower despondently.

"Not necessarily. Stay down." Seb's voice was calm. "If they're after us they could be trying every cove. Don't move. Keep right down."

"There's a boat going out on the other side. A rubber dinghy."

"Where's it going?"

"The cove. Do you think they'll find the whaler?"

"It's at the back of a cave. I tried to cover it with kelp and seaweed, but I didn't have much time. How many people in the dinghy?"

"Looks like just one, maybe two. Hang on. He's lifting the megaphone."

"Keep down!"

"I *am*," said Brian indignantly, crouching lower. "I can't see now."

"Just listen then."

A few seconds later a distorted voice came ringing out over the water.

"Sebastian Howard. Sebastian Howard. Calling Sebastian Howard."

Tim felt a fresh surge of panic.

"Don't move, anyone," whispered Seb. "Just don't move."

"Sebastian Howard, if you are on board the *Esperance*, show yourself."

They all crouched lower. Then Tim was sure he heard the sound again. A faint echo of the whale music, haunting and deep. Was it in his head or in the sea? It didn't really seem to matter.

"Show yourself now, Sebastian Howard."

Tim's heart began thumping so loudly that it was almost painful. Yet the hint of music had given him fleeting reassurance.

"I will not repeat the message. Please be aware we have three hostages on board – three members of your crew. If you don't show yourself we shall be forced to kill them. One by one."

Seb froze.

"I have one man on deck now."

"Take a look, Brian."

He crouched by the window again. "It's Scotty. He looks in a bad way."

"What kind of bad way?"

"They're holding him up. He doesn't seem able to stand."

"Unless you respond immediately this man will be thrown overboard."

"How does he *know* we're here?" hissed Tim.

"He doesn't. It's a bluff." Seb was grimly determined not to be panicked into action.

"But –"

"Relax. Wait."

"We shall be boarding you shortly. In the meantime, this man is already very ill. If you wish him to survive please show yourselves."

"Stay put."

"OK." Brian took another quick look. "I wonder what's wrong with him? Maybe they've not bothered to treat his wound properly."

"It's no good speculating." Seb was firm. "Just stay down."

"Only one thing," said Brian.

"What?"

"I can't see the dinghy any longer."

"It's probably in the cove."

"It wouldn't have had time to get there." There was an edge to Brian's voice now.

"So?"

"They could be boarding us. Now."

"Damn." Seb still didn't move. "Up the bows?"

Brian tried to crane his neck. "I just can't see."

"They'd have a damn hard job. Unless they've brought some gear."

"I couldn't see any. Wait –"

"Now what?"

"I think I can hear something. Listen."

There was silence. Then a kind of scrabbling, rasping sound. Just as Tim looked round, the bridge door, already hanging by one hinge, was abruptly kicked open.

"Stand up!" The voice was familiar, and so was the giggling laugh that accompanied it. It was June Rose.

And behind her stood a man with an automatic pistol in his hand.

Tim had never seen anyone act so quickly before. Seb leapt from his crouching position, grabbed June Rose's legs and threw her to the floor. Then, without stopping, he leapt to his feet and went for the man with the gun, punching him hard in the stomach. The man doubled up but as he did so, the gun went off, hurling Seb backwards. Meanwhile, his assailant staggered on, hands clasped to his middle until he ran into the sextant table, cracking his head on it hard.

As June Rose clambered to her feet, Flower and Brian went for her, pinning her fiercely struggling body to the floor. Tim looked from them to Seb who was clasping his arm. A dark substance was gathering on the boards below his waterproofs. Dimly Tim realized it was blood. Glancing at the man doubled up on the floor, Tim knew he had to get the gun before he came to. He ran and grabbed the revolver out of his hand. Then he went over to Seb whose face was contorted with pain.

"What happened?"

"Shot me in the arm. You got the gun? That's great, Tim. Give it to me." He put the safety catch on and then groaned. "Thank God it's only my arm. Help me bind it up. And someone stop that woman screaming."

But June Rose was thrashing and yelling on the floor with Flower and Brian still effectively pinning her down. Seb levelled the gun at the struggling heap.

"Make sure that man's still unconscious," he said to Tim. "Brian, Flower, get away from her."

They both sprang away and June Rose got to her knees.

"Stay where you are," Seb snapped.

"To hell with you." Slowly, painfully, she clambered to her feet.

Seb staggered a little. "Stay where you are," he repeated.

"I'm coming for you, Seb."

"I said, stay!"

But she was up now and walking towards him, her hands poised in karate preparation.

"Stay where you are, June."

She ignored him.

"I'm sorry." Like lightning he chopped her behind the neck with the flat of his hand and she went down without uttering a sound.

"She'll be OK. Just get them tied together."

Tying their prisoners up was rather easier said than done, given the apparent lack of appropriate materials. But eventually Seb found what looked like plastic cord in a compartment at the back of the bridge and quickly and expertly trussed their two unconscious assailants together.

"I'd better get back to the radio," he said.

"What about Stanton?" asked Brian.

"It's his move. We'll just have to play the waiting game."

And that was what it was. As June Rose and her companion slowly came round they jeered at the hopelessness of Green Watch's situation.

"Give up now," the man said. "It's only a matter of time before Stanton sends in another boarding party. You don't stand a chance."

But after an initial torrent of abuse, June Rose fell silent and merely followed them with her mad eyes. Eventually it became so oppressive on the bridge that Flower said, 'We'd better take turns to guard them. I'll stay with them for the first half-hour, then Tim, then Brian. Is that OK?"

They nodded. For a while Tim and Brian went down into the cabins and from the porthole saw with delight that the mist was slowly creeping round them again. But this time it was denser.

"This is real fog," said Tim.

The *Song of the South* was no more than a dim outline.

"The last thing we want to do is to show ourselves," said Brian. "Let them keep guessing what's happening."

"Surely they would have expected to be contacted by now?"

"Let's just do what Dad says."

"What about another boarding party though?" asked Tim anxiously.

"If we keep looking out of the portholes we should get plenty of warning. But God knows what's happening to Liam and co. I wonder how badly they've beaten them up?"

They agreed to spilt up and begin a circular tour of the ship. It was an eerie business and not at all easy,

114

for some companionways had disappeared completely and with them any ladder access. There were simply great yawning holes with the perpetual sound of lapping water beneath. But Tim kept looking out of the portholes and he was sure that no further boarding party was heading their way. Then he remembered the whales. Were they still around? He went down into the galley and listened. But there was no sound and Tim felt a hollow sense of desertion.

Towards the end of Flower's half-hour it all started happening again.

"Ahoy there!" Someone was using the megaphone, but Tim couldn't be sure whether it was Stanton this time.

"Ahoy there!"

Tim and Brian stealthily climbed up to the bridge again to find Seb looking triumphant.

"It's working," he said. "The radio's working. And I've raised Port Stanley. There's a helicopter on the way."

"That'll take a couple of hours at least," said their male guest.

June Rose laughed and a chill settled in the pit of Tim's stomach, chasing out his first rush of relief.

"Ahoy there!" came the third shout on the megaphone.

"Do we ignore them?" asked Brian irritably.

Seb nodded. "For the moment. Meanwhile, I think we'll gag our friends." He took out some oily rags from under the bridge window. "These aren't very pleasant," he said to their two prisoners, "but necessary." When he had finished, Seb looked up. "We're going to have to abandon ship," he said.

"Ahoy there!" The fourth cry was almost plaintive.

"We seem to have got them foxed." Seb grinned as he drew them down into the cabin and out of earshot of the prisoners. "But if we stay here, we're a sitting targets. We have to get back on the island, though we're in no position to outrun them – and two hours *is* a long time."

"So?" Tim's nerves were screaming. What were they doing standing here talking so casually when a boat could be coming over any minute?

"We're going to have to go back over her prow."

Tim shut his eyes. It would be an appallingly difficult descent; he was bound to fall.

"Then we'll go for the whaler, and row to another cove I know."

"But the helicopter," wailed Tim. "They won't know where to find us."

Seb's grin widened. "Oh yes, they will. I've made a rendezvous with them. Place called Seal Cove. It's the other side of the island – very obscure."

"I'll never get down that drop," said Tim, his voice breaking.

"Oh yes, you will," said Flower. "You'll climb between me and Brian. Won't he, Dad?"

Seb nodded, his eyes fixed on Tim's. "Remember what we said last time:* if your mind says you can do

* *Battle for the Badgers.*

116

it, you *can* do it. OK." Seb raised his voice slightly, looking up the ladder towards the bridge. "We'll go to the island." He picked up the radio and strapped it to his back.

Then Tim glanced out of the porthole. "It's too late," he said. "There's a boat coming."

Seb seemed completely unperturbed. "Let's go. They won't board that side; they'll need the rope like we did."

Crouching low, Seb raced up to the deck and the others followed, praying they wouldn't be seen. Luckily there was enough wreckage to conceal them. Then very quickly, too quickly for Tim, they were crowding together on the *Esperance*'s battered bow. He could see how the metal had buckled but the hand- and footholds were treacherous to say the least.

"I'll go first." Seb clambered over the drop. "Take it slowly."

Brian went after him, but Tim froze.

"OK, Tim." Flower's voice was very calm and gentle. "You helped me when I was afraid, now I'm going to help you."

But Tim wasn't listening. "Have they landed?" he gasped, his hands shaking.

"Don't worry. Just start climbing."

"I can't."

"You must."

"I just can't." He looked down at the immensity of the drop. It was impossible. He was trembling all over.

"We'll be caught." There was an urgency now in Flower's voice.

"I can't go."

"You must."

"I can't."

"Go!" She hit him hard on the face, not once but twice. Tim reeled under the blows. "*Now* go!"

Tim went.

Slowly, hand over hand, reaching down with his feet and finding they were being guided into crevices by Brian's steady hand, Tim began the descent. Flower was just above him, encouraging him.

"That's right, just there. Terrific, Tim. You've gone a long way already. Let Brian steady the foot. OK, Brian? Great Tim, you're doing super. Really great. Watch that hand. You've got it."

She never stopped talking, issuing a stream of instructions and praise. Slowly, but more surely, Tim found himself climbing down, his hands and feet trembling but a tiny degree of confidence beginning to build up inside him.

"OK. You're halfway now. Not far to go; you've done the worst. Get that foot locked in, and your hands free. You've got a really good grip there."

A few minutes later Tim was standing on damp, solid, wonderful sand.

As Flower jumped down beside him, she said, "Sorry."

"Eh?"

"For hitting you."

"Oh, that. I was just behaving like a baby." He felt elated but ashamed.

"Rubbish. It was tough."

"Thanks anyway. I needed it."

Seb came up to them. "We have to get to the whaler, or are you going to spend the rest of the day chatting?"

"Come on," said Brian. "Let's get some cover."

They began to run towards the cliffs.

"Here she is. Get her in the water fast."

They yanked the whaler out of the cave and five minutes later, utterly exhausted, they had her in the shallows. They jumped in from the ice-cold water, and Seb and Flower took the oars and began to pull as hard as they could. Ten minutes later, they were making some progress along the coast but to Tim it still seemed frustratingly slow.

Then Brian said quietly, "They're coming."

Darting a glance over his shoulder, Tim saw the rubber dinghy. There were two people in it: Stanton and June Rose. She had something in her hand. Tim knew it was a gun.

"We've had it," he muttered.

"Keep rowing," yelled Seb and Flower tried to redouble her efforts.

"She's going to fire at us," said Brian.

"I've got the film; they'd be taking too much of a risk. If this boat overturns –"

"We'll die in a few seconds," remarked Brian almost as if he were talking about characters in a film.

"If we die the film's destroyed anyway," he added with icy logic.

"They won't try anything now," replied Seb stubbornly.

There was a crack and a shot whistled past them.

"Famous last words, Dad?" panted Flower.

"She's firing over our heads. Don't let it worry you."

"Oh no," said Tim bleakly, "I'm not worried."

They rowed on and another shot rang out. It seemed lower this time.

"Keep rowing," snapped Seb.

"What do you think I'm doing?" raged Flower. "Boiling an egg?"

"Blimey." Tim had seen a sudden churning in the water behind them.

"It's a whale," said Brian slowly. "It must have been frightened by the shots."

But it wasn't just one whale. Other eruptions burst out of the water and spume flew in the mist. There were three – no four – that Tim could count. The effect on June Rose was immediate. They could hear her screaming, hear Stanton's voice trying to calm her.

"Keep rowing," shouted Seb. "Whatever you do, keep rowing."

The whales glided through the swell, and as the dinghy gained on them, one of the whales seemed to close in. It was only the slightest of movements but it had June Rose standing up, screaming at Stanton.

She still had the gun and was waving it at him.

"Turn round! Get away from them!"

"Don't be a damn fool!"

"I'll kill you if you don't turn round."

"We'll lose them – we'll lose the film."

"The whales'll kill us. Like they killed –" She had burst into hard dry sobs. "Go back," she screamed. "Now!"

Two more shots rang out in quick succession and looking round, Tim saw Stanton gasp, clutching at his arm.

"You bloody fool!"

"Turn round. If you don't I'll kill you next time."

Viciously Stanton turned the helm with his uninjured arm and the rubber dinghy vanished into the mist.

The whales rode alongside them for another few minutes. Then above their heads, Green Watch could hear the clattering of a helicopter. It swooped low out of the mist and Tim could see somone waving.

"We're OK now," Seb cried. "Thank God! We're OK. And they won't hurt Liam and the others now."

The whales, frightened by the noise of the helicopter, dived, and the whaler rocked ominously. But they didn't capsize and Seb and Flower, arms aching, carried on rowing for the little cove. Tim had never experienced such a glorious feeling of relief.

"We've done it," he said, punching Brian's

shoulder with his fist. "We've done it, we've beaten them."

"Full credit to the whales," replied Brian.

Tim looked down at the grey-green swell. Somewhere down there he knew they were singing.

Epilogue
Two weeks later

Seb, Brian, Flower and Tim sat round the table with the map of the world drawn so delicately at its centre. This was the Green Watch headquarters, the Howard family's converted windmill on the Romney Marshes. It was raining steadily, but in the cosy room there was a general glow of satisfaction. On the table lay a pile of newspapers and the most prominent headlines read:

GREEN FAMILY BOARD FACTORY SHIP
DEADLY HARPOON GUN FOUND
WHALES THREATENED BY POISON
INTERNATIONAL WHALING PROTESTS

"Will it do any good, that's the point?" asked Brian. Seb shook his head. "I just don't know. We've done all we could. We've made one hell of a fuss, and drawn it to public attention."

"Do you reckon they'll still carry on, Dad?"

"Whaling? Yes. And we'll go on campaigning – just as the other groups will. June's horrible invention? I don't know. I think it's unlikely."

"Will there be any whales left eventually?" Tim was close to tears. Could everything they had done – everything they had been through – count for nothing in the end?

"There won't be if the killing goes on at this rate." Seb spoke very slowly. "But there *is* protection now. Providing the law isn't broken – which I'm afraid it very often is."

"It would be dreadful, wouldn't it?" said Flower. "If we never heard that song again."

That sad, happy, mysterious song, thought Tim. He gazed out into the rain, and inside his head he could hear the whales calling still.